G. K. Chesterton

THE NAPOLEON OF
NOTTING HILL

THE BODLEY HEAD

LONDON · SYDNEY
TORONTO

SBN 370 00578 3

Printed in Great Britain for
THE BODLEY HEAD LTD
9 Bow Street, London WC2
by Lowe & Brydone (Printers) Ltd, London

First published 1904
Twelfth impression 1968

THE NAPOLEON OF NOTTING HILL

by the same author

HERETICS
GEORGE BERNARD SHAW
ORTHODOXY

TO HILAIRE BELLOC

For every tiny town or place
God made the stars especially;
Babies look up with owlish face
And see them tangled in a tree;
You saw a moon from Sussex Downs,
A Sussex moon, untravelled still,
I saw a moon that was the town's,
The largest lamp on Campden Hill.

Yea; Heaven is everywhere at home
The big blue cap that always fits,
And so it is (be calm; they come
To goal at last, my wandering wits),
So is it with the heroic thing;
This shall not end for the world's end
And though the sullen engines swing,
Be you not much afraid, my friend.

This did not end by Nelson's urn
Where an immortal England sits—
Nor where your tall young men in turn
Drank death like wine at Austerlitz.
And when the pedants bade us mark
What cold mechanic happenings
Must come; our souls said in the dark,
'Belike; but there are likelier things.'

Likelier across these flats afar
These sulky levels smooth and free
The drums shall crash a waltz of war
And Death shall dance with Liberty;
Likelier the barricades shall blare
Slaughter below and smoke above,
And death and hate and hell declare
That men have found a thing to love.

Far from your sunny uplands set
I saw the dream; the streets I trod
The lit straight streets shot out and met
The starry streets that point to God.
This legend of an epic hour
A child I dreamed, and dream it still,
Under the great grey water-tower
That strikes the stars on Campden Hill.

G. K. C.

CONTENTS

BOOK ONE

BOOK TWO

BOOK THREE

BOOK FOUR

BOOK FIVE

BOOK ONE

★

CHAPTER I

Introductory Remarks on
the Art of Prophecy

THE human race, to which so many of my readers belong,
has been playing at children's games from the beginning,
and will probably do it till the end, which is a nuisance for
the few people who grow up. And one of the games to
which it is most attached is called, 'Keep to-morrow
dark,' and which is also named (by the rustics in Shrop-
shire, I have no doubt) 'Cheat the Prophet.' The players
listen very carefully and respectfully to all that the clever
men have to say about what is to happen in the next generation. The players then wait until all the clever men are
dead, and bury them nicely. They then go and do something else. That is all. For a race of simple tastes, however,
it is great fun.

For human beings, being children, have the childish
wilfulness and the childish secrecy. And they never have
from the beginning of the world done what the wise men
have seen to be inevitable. They stoned the false prophets,
it is said; but they could have stoned true prophets with a
greater and juster enjoyment. Individually, men may present a more or less rational appearance, eating, sleeping, and
scheming. But humanity as a whole is changeful, mystical,
fickle, delightful. Men are men, but Man is a woman.

But in the beginning of the twentieth century the game
of Cheat the Prophet was made far more difficult than it

had ever been before. The reason was, that there were so many prophets and so many prophecies, that it was difficult to elude all their ingenuities. When a man did something free and frantic and entirely his own, a horrible thought struck him afterwards; it might have been predicted. Whenever a duke climbed a lamp-post, when a dean got drunk, he could not be really happy, he could not be certain that he was not fulfilling some prophecy. In the beginning of the twentieth century you could not see the ground for clever men. They were so common that a stupid man was quite exceptional, and when they found him, they followed him in crowds down the street and treasured him up and gave him some high post in the State. And all these clever men were at work giving accounts of what would happen in the next age, all quite clear, all quite keen-sighted and ruthless, and all quite different. And it seemed that the good old game of hoodwinking your ancestors could not really be managed this time, because the ancestors neglected meat and sleep and practical politics, so that they might meditate day and night on what their descendants would be likely to do.

But the way the prophets of the twentieth century went to work was this. They took something or other that was certainly going on in their time, and then said that it would go on more and more until something extraordinary happened. And very often they added that in some odd place that extraordinary thing had happened, and that it showed the signs of the times.

Thus, for instance, there were Mr. H. G. Wells and others, who thought that science would take charge of the future; and just as the motor-car was quicker than the coach, so some lovely thing would be quicker than the motor-car; and so on for ever. And there arose from their ashes Dr. Quilp, who said that a man could be sent on his machine so fast round the world that he could keep up a long chatty conversation in some old-world village by saying a word of a sentence each time he came round. And it was said that the experiment had been tried on an apoplectic old major, who was sent round the world so fast that there seemed to be (to the inhabitants of some other star) a continuous band round the earth of white whiskers, red complexion and tweeds—a thing like the ring of Saturn.

Then there was the opposite school. There was Mr. Edward Carpenter, who thought we should in a very short time return to Nature, and live simply and slowly as the animals do. And Edward Carpenter was followed by James Pickie, D.D. (of Pocahontas College), who said that men were immensely improved by grazing, or taking their food slowly and continuously, after the manner of cows. And he said that he had, with the most encouraging results, turned city men out on all fours in a field covered with veal cutlets. Then Tolstoy and the Humanitarians said that the world was growing more merciful, and therefore no one would ever desire to kill. And Mr. Mick not only became a vegetarian, but at length declared vegetarianism doomed ('shedding,' as he called it finely, 'the green blood of the silent animals'), and predicted that men in a better age would live on nothing but salt. And then came the pamphlet from Oregon (where the thing was tried), the pamphlet called 'Why should Salt suffer?' and there was more trouble.

And on the other hand, some people were predicting that the lines of kinship would become narrower and sterner. There was Mr. Cecil Rhodes, who thought that the one thing of the future was the British Empire, and that there would be a gulf between those who were of the Empire and those who were not, between the Chinaman in Hong Kong and the Chinaman outside, between the Spaniard on the Rock of Gibraltar and the Spaniard off it, similar to the gulf between man and the lower animals. And in the same way his impetuous friend, Dr. Zoppi ('the Paul of Anglo-Saxonism'), carried it yet further, and held that, as a result of this view, cannibalism should be held to mean eating a member of the Empire, not eating one of the subject peoples, who should, he said, be killed without needless pain. His horror at the idea of eating a man in British Guiana showed how they misunderstood his stoicism who thought him devoid of feeling. He was, however, in a hard position; as it was said that he had attempted the experiment, and, living in London, had to subsist entirely on Italian organ-grinders. And his end was terrible, for just when he had begun, Sir Paul Swiller read his great paper at the Royal Society, proving that the savages were not only quite right in eating their enemies, but right on moral and hygienic grounds, since it was true that the qualities of the enemy, when eaten, passed into the eater. The notion that the nature of an Italian organ-man was irrevocably growing and burgeoning inside him was almost more than the kindly old professor could bear.

There was Mr. Benjamin Kidd, who said that the growing note of our race would be the care for and knowledge of the future. His idea was developed more powerfully by William Borker, who wrote that passage which every schoolboy knows by heart, about men in future ages weeping by the graves of their descendants, and tourists being shown over the scene of the historic battle which was to take place some centuries afterwards.

And Mr. Stead, too, was prominent, who thought that England would in the twentieth century be united to America; and his young lieutenant, Graham Podge, who included the states of France, Germany, and Russia in the American Union, the State of Russia being abbreviated to Ra.

There was Mr. Sidney Webb, also, who said that the future would see a continuously increasing order and neatness in the life of the people, and his poor friend Fipps, who went mad and ran about the country with an axe, hacking branches off the trees whenever there were not the same number on both sides.

All these clever men were prophesying with every variety of ingenuity what would happen soon, and they all did it in the same way, by taking something they saw 'going strong,' as the saying is, and carrying it as far as ever their imagination could stretch. This, they said, was the true and simple way of anticipating the future. 'Just as,' said Dr. Pellkins, in a fine passage—'just as when we see a pig in a litter larger than the other pigs, we know that by an unalterable law of the Inscrutable it will some day be larger than an elephant—just as we know, when we see weeds and dandelions growing more and more thickly in a garden, that they must, in spite of all our efforts, grow taller than the chimney-pots and swallow the house from sight, so we know and reverently acknowledge, that when any power in human politics has shown for any period of time any considerable activity, it will go on until it reaches to the sky.'

And it did certainly appear that the prophets had put the

people (engaged in the old game of Cheat the Prophet) in a quite unprecedented difficulty. It seemed really hard to do anything without fulfilling some of their prophecies.

But there was, nevertheless, in the eyes of labourers in the streets, of peasants in the fields, of sailors and children, and especially women, a strange look that kept the wise men in a perfect fever of doubt. They could not fathom the motionless mirth in their eyes. They still had something up their sleeve; they were still playing the game of Cheat the Prophet.

Then the wise men grew like wild things, and swayed hither and thither, crying 'What can it be? What can it be? What will London be like a century hence? Is there anything we have not thought of? Houses upside down— more hygienic, perhaps? Men walking on hands—make feet flexible, don't you know? Moon . . . motor-cars . . . no heads. . . .' And so they swayed and wondered until they died and were buried nicely.

Then the people went and did what they liked. Let me no longer conceal the painful truth. The people had cheated the prophets of the twentieth century. When the curtain goes up on this story, eighty years after the present date, London is almost exactly like what it is now.

CHAPTER II

The Man in Green

VERY few words are needed to explain why London, a hundred years hence, will be very like it is now, or rather, since I must slip into a prophetic past, why London, when my story opens, was very like it was in those enviable days when I was still alive.

The reason can be stated in one sentence. The people had absolutely lost faith in revolutions. All revolutions are doctrinal—such as the French one, or the one that introduced Christianity. For it stands to common sense that you cannot upset all existing things, customs, and compromises, unless you believe in something outside them, something positive and divine. Now, England, during this century, lost all belief in this. It believed in a thing called Evolution. And it said, 'All theoretic changes have ended in blood and ennui. If we change, we must change slowly and safely, as the animals do. Nature's revolutions are the only successful ones. There has been no conservative reaction in favour of tails.'

And some things did change. Things that were not much thought of dropped out of sight. Things that had not often happened did not happen at all. Thus, for instance, the actual physical force ruling the country, the soldiers and police, grew smaller and smaller, and at last vanished almost to a point. The people combined could have swept the few policemen away in ten minutes: they did not, because they did not believe it would do them the least good. They had lost faith in revolutions.

Democracy was dead; for no one minded the governing class governing. England was now practically a despotism, but not an hereditary one. Some one in the official class was made King. No one cared how: no one cared who. He was merely an universal secretary.

In this manner it happened that everything in London was very quiet. That vague and somewhat depressed reliance upon things happening as they have always happened, which is with all Londoners a mood, had become an assumed condition. There was really no reason for any man doing anything but the thing he had done the day before.

There was therefore no reason whatever why the three young men who had always walked up to their Government office together should not walk up to it together on this particular wintry and cloudy morning. Everything in that age had become mechanical, and Government clerks especially. All those clerks assembled regularly at their posts. Three of those clerks always walked into town together. All the neighbourhood knew them: two of them were tall and one short. And on this particular morning the short clerk was only a few seconds late to join the other two as they passed his gate: he could have overtaken them in three strides; he could have called after them easily. But he did not.

For some reason that will never be understood until all souls are judged (if they are ever judged; the idea was at this time classed with fetish worship) he did not join his two companions, but walked steadily behind them. The day was dull, their dress was dull, everything was dull; but in some odd impulse he walked through street after street, through district after district, looking at the backs of the

two men, who would have swung round at the sound of
his voice. Now, there is a law written in the darkest of the
Books of Life, and it is this: If you look at a thing nine
hundred and ninety-nine times, you are perfectly safe; if
you look at it the thousandth time, you are in frightful
danger of seeing it for the first time.

So the short Government official looked at the coat-tails
of the tall Government officials, and through street after
street, and round corner after corner, saw only coat-tails,
coat-tails, and again coat-tails—when, he did not in the
least know why, something happened to his eyes.

Two black dragons were walking backwards in front of
him. Two black dragons were looking at him with evil
eyes. The dragons were walking backwards it was true,
but they kept their eyes fixed on him none the less. The
eyes which he saw were, in truth, only the two buttons at
the back of a frock-coat: perhaps some traditional memory
of their meaningless character gave this half-witted pro-
minence to their gaze. The slit between the tails was the
nose-line of the monster: whenever the tails flapped in the
winter wind the dragons licked their lips. It was only a
momentary fancy, but the small clerk found it imbedded
in his soul ever afterwards. He never could again think of
men in frock-coats except as dragons walking backwards.
He explained afterwards, quite tactfully and nicely, to his
two official friends, that while feeling an inexpressible
regard for each of them he could not seriously regard the
face of either of them as anything but a kind of tail. It was,
he admitted, a handsome tail—a tail elevated in the air.
But if, he said, any true friend of theirs wished to see their
faces, to look into the eyes of their soul, that friend must be
allowed to walk reverently round behind them, so as to see

them from the rear. There he would see the two black dragons with the blind eyes.

But when first the two black dragons sprang out of the fog upon the small clerk, they had merely the effect of all miracles—they changed the universe. He discovered the fact that all romantics know—that adventures happen on dull days, and not on sunny ones. When the chord of monotony is stretched most tight, then it breaks with a sound like song. He had scarcely noticed the weather before, but with the four dead eyes glaring at him he looked round and realised the strange dead day.

The morning was wintry and dim, not misty, but darkened with that shadow of cloud or snow which steeps everything in a green or copper twilight. The light there is on such a day seems not so much to come from the clear heavens as to be a phosphorescence clinging to the shapes themselves. The load of heaven and the clouds is like a load of waters, and the men move like fishes, feeling that they are on the floor of a sea. Everything in a London street completes the fantasy; the carriages and cabs themselves resemble deep-sea creatures with eyes of flame. He had been startled at first to meet two dragons. Now he found he was among deep-sea dragons possessing the deep sea.

The two young men in front were like the small young man himself, well-dressed. The lines of their frock-coats and silk hats had that luxuriant severity which makes the modern fop, hideous as he is, a favourite exercise of the modern draughtsman; that element which Mr. Max Beerbohm has admirably expressed in speaking of 'certain congruities of dark cloth and the rigid perfection of linen.'

They walked with the gait of an affected snail, and they

spoke at the longest intervals, dropping a sentence at about every sixth lamp-post.

They crawled on past the lamp-posts; their mien was so immovable that a fanciful description might almost say, that the lamp-posts crawled past the men, as in a dream. Then the small man suddenly ran after them and said—

'I want to get my hair cut. I say, do you know a little shop anywhere where they cut your hair properly? I keep on having my hair cut, but it keeps on growing again.'

One of the tall men looked at him with the air of a pained naturalist.

'Why, here is a little place,' cried the small man, with a sort of imbecile cheerfulness, as the bright bulging window of a fashionable toilet-saloon glowed abruptly out of the foggy twilight. 'Do you know, I often find hairdressers when I walk about London. I'll lunch with you at Cicconani's. You know, I'm awfully fond of hairdressers' shops. They're miles better than those nasty butchers'.' And he disappeared into the doorway.

The man called James continued to gaze after him, a monocle screwed into his eyes.

'What the devil do you make of that fellow?' he asked his companion, a pale young man with a high nose.

The pale young man reflected conscientiously for some minutes, and then said—

'Had a knock on his head when he was a kid, I should think.'

'No, I don't think it's that,' replied the Honourable James Barker. 'I've sometimes fancied he was a sort of artist, Lambert.'

'Bosh!' cried Mr. Lambert, briefly.

'I admit I can't make him out,' resumed Barker, abstractedly; 'he never opens his mouth without saying something so indescribably half-witted that to call him a fool seems the very feeblest attempt at characterisation. But there's another thing about him that's rather funny. Do you know that he has the one collection of Japanese lacquer in Europe? Have you ever seen his books? All Greek poets and mediæval French and that sort of thing. Have you ever been in his rooms? It's like being inside an amethyst. And he moves about in all that and talks like—like a turnip.'

'Well, damn all books. Your blue books as well,' said the ingenuous Mr. Lambert, with a friendly simplicity. 'You ought to understand such things. What do you make of him?'

'He's beyond me,' returned Barker. 'But if you asked me for my opinion, I should say he was a man with a taste for nonsense, as they call it—artistic fooling, and all that kind of thing. And I seriously believe that he has talked nonsense so much that he has half bewildered his own mind and doesn't know the difference between sanity and insanity. He has gone round the mental world, so to speak, and found the place where the East and the West are one, and extreme idiocy is as good as sense. But I can't explain these psychological games.'

'You can't explain them to me,' replied Mr. Wilfrid Lambert, with candour.

As they passed up the long streets towards their restaurant the copper twilight cleared slowly to a pale yellow, and by the time they reached it they stood discernible in a tolerable winter daylight. The Honourable James Barker, one of the most powerful officials in the English Government (by this time a rigidly official one), was a lean and elegant young man, with a blank handsome face and bleak blue eyes. He had a great amount of intellectual capacity, of that peculiar kind which raises a man from throne to throne and lets him die loaded with honours without having either amused or enlightened the mind of a single man. Wilfrid Lambert, the youth with the nose which appeared to impoverish the rest of his face, had also contributed little to the enlargement of the human spirit, but he had the honourable excuse of being a fool.

Lambert would have been called a silly man; Barker, with all his cleverness, might have been called a stupid man. But mere silliness and stupidity sank into insignificance in the presence of the awful and mysterious treasurers of foolishness apparently stored up in the small figure that stood waiting for them outside Cicconani's. The little man, whose name was Auberon Quin, had an appearance compounded of a baby and an owl. His round head, round eyes, seemed to have been designed by nature playfully with a pair of compasses. His flat dark hair and preposterously long frock-coat gave him something of the look of a child's 'Noah.' When he entered a room of strangers, they mistook him for a small boy, and wanted to take him on their knees, until he spoke, when they perceived that a boy would have been more intelligent.

'I have been waiting quite a long time,' said Quin, mildly. 'It's awfully funny I should see you coming up the street at last.'

'Why?' asked Lambert, staring. 'You told us to come here yourself.'

'My mother used to tell people to come to places,' said the sage.

They were about to turn into the restaurant with a

resigned air, when their eyes were caught by something in
the street. The weather, though cold and blank, was now
quite clear and across the dull brown of the wood pavement
and between the dull grey terraces was moving something
not to be seen for miles around—not to be seen perhaps at
that time in England—a man dressed in bright colours. A
small crowd hung on the man's heels.

He was a tall stately man, clad in a military uniform of
brilliant green, splashed with great silver facings. From the
shoulder swung a short green furred cloak, somewhat like
that of a Hussar, the lining of which gleamed every now
and then with a kind of tawny crimson. His breast glittered
with medals; round his neck was the red ribbon and star
of some foreign order; and a long straight sword, with a
blazing hilt, trailed and clattered along the pavement. At
this time the pacific and utilitarian development of Europe
had relegated all such customs to the Museums. The only
remaining force, the small but well-organised police, were
attired in a sombre and hygienic manner. But even those
who remembered the last Life Guards and Lancers who disappeared in 1912 must have known at a glance that this was
not, and never had been, an English uniform; and this con-
viction would have been heightened by the yellow aquiline
face, like Dante carved in bronze, which rose, crowned
with white hair, out of the green military collar, a keen and
distinguished, but not an English face.

The magnificence with which the green-clad gentleman
walked down the centre of the road would be something
difficult to express in human language. For it was an ingrained simplicity and arrogance, something in the mere
carriage of the head and body, which made ordinary
moderns in the street stare after him; but it had compara-

tively little to do with actual conscious gestures or expression. In the matter of these merely temporary movements, the man appeared to be rather worried and inquisitive, but he was inquisitive with the inquisitiveness of a despot and worried as with the responsibilities of a god. The men who lounged and wondered behind him followed partly with an astonishment at his brilliant uniform, that is to say, partly because of that instinct which makes us all follow one who looks like a madman, but far more because of that instinct which makes all men follow (and worship) any one who chooses to behave like a king. He had to so sublime an extent that great quality of royalty—an almost imbecile unconsciousness of everybody, that people went after him as they do after kings—to see what would be the first thing or person he would take notice of. And all the time, as we have said, in spite of his quiet splendour, there was an air about him as if he were looking for somebody; an expression of inquiry.

Suddenly that expression of inquiry vanished, none could tell why, and was replaced by an expression of contentment. Amid the rapt attention of the mob of idlers, the magnificent green gentleman deflected himself from his direct course down the centre of the road and walked to one side of it. He came to a halt opposite to a large poster of Colman's Mustard erected on a wooden hoarding. His spectators almost held their breath.

He took from a small pocket in his uniform a little penknife; with this he made a slash at the stretched paper. Completing the rest of the operation with his fingers, he tore off a strip or rag of paper, yellow in colour and wholly irregular in outline. Then for the first time the great being addressed his adoring onlookers—

'Can any one,' he said, with a pleasing foreign accent, 'lend me a pin?'

Mr. Lambert, who happened to be nearest, and who carried innumerable pins for the purpose of attaching innumerable buttonholes, lent him one, which was received with extravagant but dignified bows, and hyperboles of thanks.

The gentleman in green, then, with every appearance of being gratified, and even puffed up, pinned the piece of yellow paper to the green silk and silver-lace adornments of his breast. Then he turned his eyes round again, searching and unsatisfied.

'Anything else I can do, sir?' asked Lambert, with the absurd politeness of the Englishman when once embarrassed.

'Red,' said the stranger, vaguely, 'red.'

'I beg your pardon?'

'I beg yours also, Senor,' said the stranger, bowing. 'I was wondering whether any of you had any red about you.'

'Any red about us?—well really—no, I don't think I have—I used to carry a red bandanna once, but——'

'Barker,' asked Auberon Quin, suddenly, 'where's your red cockatoo? Where's your red cockatoo?'

'What do you mean?' asked Barker, desperately. 'What cockatoo? You've never seen me with any cockatoo.'

'I know,' said Auberon, vaguely mollified. 'Where's it been all the time?'

Barker swung round, not without resentment.

'I am sorry, sir,' he said, shortly but civilly, 'none of us seem to have anything red to lend you. But why, if one may ask——'

'I thank you, Senor, it is nothing. I can, since there is nothing else, fulfil my own requirements.'

And standing for a second of thought with the penknife in his hand, he stabbed his left palm. The blood fell with so full a stream that it struck the stones without dripping. The foreigner pulled out his handkerchief and tore a piece from it with his teeth. The rag was immediately soaked in scarlet.

'Since you are so generous, Senor,' he said, 'another pin, perhaps.'

Lambert held one out, with eyes protruding like a frog's.

The red linen was pinned beside the yellow paper, and the foreigner took off his hat.

'I have to thank you all, gentlemen,' he said; and wrapping the remainder of the handkerchief round his bleeding hand, he resumed his walk with an overwhelming stateliness.

While all the rest paused, in some disorder, little Mr. Auberon Quin ran after the stranger and stopped him, with hat in hand. Considerably to everybody's astonishment, he addressed him in the purest Spanish—

'Senor,' he said in that language, 'pardon a hospitality, perhaps indiscreet, towards one who appears to be a distinguished, but a solitary guest in London. Will you do me and my friends, with whom you have held some conversation, the honour of lunching with us at the adjoining restaurant?'

The man in the green uniform had turned a fiery colour of pleasure at the mere sound of his own language, and he accepted the invitation with that profusion of bows which so often shows, in the case of the Southern races, the false-hood of the notion that ceremony has nothing to do with feeling.

'Senor,' he said, 'your language is my own; but all my

love for my people shall not lead me to deny to yours the possession of so chivalrous an entertainer. Let me say that the tongue is Spanish but the heart English.' And he passed with the rest into Cicconani's.

'Now, perhaps,' said Barker, over the fish and sherry, intensely polite, but burning with curiosity, 'perhaps it would be rude of me to ask why you did that?'

'Did what, Senor?' asked the guest, who spoke English quite well, though in a manner indefinably American.

'Well,' said the Englishman, in some confusion, 'I mean tore a strip off a hoarding and . . . er . . . cut yourself . . . and. . . .'

'To tell you that, Senor,' answered the other, with a certain sad pride, 'involves merely telling you who I am. I am Juan del Fuego, President of Nicaragua.'

The manner with which the President of Nicaragua leant back and drank his sherry showed that to him this explanation covered all the facts observed and a great deal more. Barker's brow, however, was still a little clouded.

'And the yellow paper,' he began, with anxious friendliness, 'and the red rag. . . .'

'The yellow paper and the red rag,' said Fuego, with indescribable grandeur, 'are the colours of Nicaragua.'

'But Nicaragua. . . .' began Barker, with great hesitation, 'Nicaragua is no longer a. . . ."

'Nicaragua has been conquered like Athens. Nicaragua has been annexed like Jerusalem,' cried the old man, with amazing fire. 'The Yankee and the German and the brute powers of modernity have trampled it with the hoofs of oxen. But Nicaragua is not dead. Nicaragua is an idea.'

Auberon Quin suggested timidly, 'A brilliant idea.'

'Yes,' said the foreigner, snatching at the word. 'You

are right, generous Englishman. An idea *brilliant*, a burning thought. Senor, you asked me why, in my desire to see the colours of my country, I snatched at paper and blood. Can you not understand the ancient sanctity of colours? The Church has her symbolic colours. And think of what colours mean to us—think of the position of one like myself, who can see nothing but those two colours, nothing but the red and the yellow. To me all shapes are equal, all common and noble things are in a democracy of combination. Wherever there is a field of marigolds and the red cloak of an old woman, there is Nicaragua. Wherever there is a field of poppies and a yellow patch of sand, there is Nicaragua. Wherever there is a lemon and a red sunset, there is my country. Wherever I see a red pillar-box and a yellow sunset, there my heart beats. Blood and a splash of mustard can be my heraldry. If there be yellow mud and red mud in the same ditch, it is better to me than white stars.'

'And if,' said Quin, with equal enthusiasm, 'there should happen to be yellow wine and red wine at the same lunch, you could not confine yourself to sherry. Let me order some Burgundy, and complete, as it were, a sort of Nicaraguan heraldry in your inside.'

Barker was fiddling with his knife, and was evidently making up his mind to say something, with the intense nervousness of the amiable Englishman.

'I am to understand, then,' he said at last, with a cough, 'that you, ahem, were the President of Nicaragua when it made its—er—one must, of course, agree—its quite heroic resistance to—er——'

The ex-President of Nicaragua waved his hand.

'You need not hesitate in speaking to me,' he said. 'I am

quite fully aware that the whole tendency of the world of to-day is against Nicaragua and against me. I shall not consider it any diminution of your evident courtesy if you say what you think of the misfortunes that have laid my republic in ruins.'

Barker looked immeasurably relieved and gratified.

'You are most generous, President,' he said, with some hesitation over the title, 'and I will take advantage of your generosity to express the doubts which, I must confess, we moderns have about such things as—er—the Nicaraguan independence.'

'So your sympathies are,' said Del Fuego, quite calmly, 'with the big nation which——'

'Pardon me, pardon me, President,' said Barker, warmly; 'my sympathies are with no nation. You misunderstand, I think, the modern intellect. We do not disapprove of the fire and extravagance of such commonwealths as yours only to become more extravagant on a larger scale. We do not condemn Nicaragua because we think Britain ought to be more Nicaraguan. We do not discourage small nationalities because we wish large nationalities to have all their smallness, all their uniformity of outlook, all their exaggeration of spirit. If I differ with the greatest respect from your Nicaraguan enthusiasm, it is not because a nation or ten nations were against you; it is because civilisation was against you. We moderns believe in a great cosmopolitan civilisation, one which shall include all the talents of all the absorbed peoples——'

'The Senor will forgive me,' said the President. 'May I ask the Senor how, under ordinary circumstances, he catches a wild horse?'

'I never catch a wild horse,' replied Barker, with dignity.

'Precisely,' said the other; 'and there ends your absorption of the talents. That is what I complain of your cosmopolitanism. When you say you want all peoples to unite, you really mean that you want all peoples to unite to learn the tricks of your people. If the Bedouin Arab does not know how to read, some English missionary or schoolmaster must be sent to teach him to read, but no one ever says, "This schoolmaster does not know how to ride on a camel; let us pay a Bedouin to teach him." You say your civilisation will include all talents. Will it? Do you really mean to say that at the moment when the Esquimaux has learnt to vote for a County Council, you will have learnt to spear a walrus? I recur to the example I gave. In Nicaragua we had a way of catching wild horses—by lassooing the fore feet—which was supposed to be the best in South America. If you are going to include all the talents, go and do it. If not, permit me to say, what I have always said, that something went from the world when Nicaragua was civilised.'

'Something, perhaps,' replied Barker, 'but that something a mere barbarian dexterity. I do not know that I could chip flints as well as a primeval man, but I know that civilisation can make these knives which are better, and I trust to civilisation.'

'You have good authority,' answered the Nicaraguan. 'Many clever men like you have trusted to civilisation. Many clever Babylonians, many clever Egyptians, many clever men at the end of Rome. Can you tell me, in a world that is flagrant with the failures of civilisation, what there is particularly immortal about yours?'

'I think you do not quite understand, President, what ours is,' answered Barker. 'You judge it rather as if England was still a poor and pugnacious island; you have been long out of Europe. Many things have happened.'

'And what,' asked the other, 'would you call the summary of those things?'

'The summary of those things,' answered Barker, with great animation, 'is that we are rid of the superstitions, and in becoming so we have not merely become rid of the superstitions which have been most frequently and most enthusiastically so described. The superstition of big nationalities is bad, but the superstition of small nationalities is worse. The superstition of reverencing our own country is bad, but the superstition of reverencing other people's countries is worse. It is so everywhere, and in a hundred ways. The superstition of monarchy is bad, and the superstition of aristocracy is bad, but the superstition of democracy is the worst of all.'

The old gentleman opened his eyes with some surprise.

'Are you, then,' he said, 'no longer a democracy in England?'

Barker laughed.

'The situation invites paradox,' he said. 'We are, in a sense, the purest democracy. We have become a despotism. Have you not noticed how continually in history democracy becomes despotism? People call it the decay of democracy. It is simply its fulfilment. Why take the trouble to number and register and enfranchise all the innumerable John Robinsons, when you can take one John Robinson with the same intellect or lack of intellect as all the rest, and have done with it? The old idealistic republicans used to found democracy on the idea that all men were equally intelligent. Believe me, the sane and enduring democracy is founded on the fact that all men are equally idiotic. Why should we not choose out of them one as much as another? All that we want for Government is a man not criminal and insane, who can rapidly look over some petitions and sign some proclamations. To think what time was wasted in arguing about the House of Lords, Tories saying it ought to be preserved because it was clever, and Radicals saying it ought to be destroyed because it was stupid, and all the time no one saw that it was right because it was stupid, because that chance mob of ordinary men thrown there by accident of blood, were a great democratic protest against the Lower House, against the eternal insolence of the aristocracy of talents. We have established now in England, the thing towards which all systems have dimly groped, the dull popular despotism without illusions. We want one man at the head of our State, not because he is brilliant or virtuous, but because he is one man and not a chattering crowd. To avoid the possible chance of hereditary diseases or such things, we have abandoned hereditary monarchy. The King of England is chosen like a juryman upon an official rotation list. Beyond that the whole system is quietly despotic, and we have not found it raise a murmur.'

'Do you really mean,' asked the President, incredulously, 'that you choose any ordinary man that comes to hand and make him despot—that you trust to the chance of some alphabetical list. . . .'

'And why not?' cried Barker. 'Did not half the historical nations trust to the chance of the eldest sons of eldest sons, and did not half of them get on tolerably well? To have a perfect system is impossible; to have a system is indispensable. All hereditary monarchies were a matter of luck; so are alphabetical monarchies. Can you find a deep philosophical meaning in the difference between the Stuarts

and the Hanoverians? Believe me, I will undertake to find
a deep philosophical meaning in the contrast between the
dark tragedy of the A's, and the solid success of the B's.'

'And you risk it?' asked the other. 'Though the man
may be a tyrant or a cynic or a criminal?'

'We risk it,' answered Barker, with a perfect placidity.
'Suppose he is a tyrant—he is still a check on a hundred
tyrants. Suppose he is a cynic, it is to his interest to govern
well. Suppose he is a criminal—by removing poverty and
substituting power, we put a check on his criminality. In
short, by substituting despotism we have put a total check
on one criminal and a partial check on all the rest.'

The Nicaraguan old gentleman leaned over with a queer
expression in his eyes.

'My church, sir,' he said, 'has taught me to respect faith.
I do not wish to speak with any disrespect of yours, however fantastic. But do you really mean that you will trust
to the ordinary man, the man who may happen to come
next, as a good despot?'

'I do,' said Barker, simply. 'He may not be a good man.
But he will be a good despot. For when he comes to a mere
business routine of government he will endeavour to do
ordinary justice. Do we not assume the same thing in a
jury?'

The old President smiled.

'I don't know,' he said, 'that I have any particular objection in detail to your excellent scheme of Government. My
only objection is a quite personal one. It is, that if I were
asked whether I would belong to it, I should ask first of all,
if I was not permitted, as an alternative, to be a toad in a
ditch. That is all. You cannot argue with the choice of the
soul.'

'Of the soul,' said Barker, knitting his brows, 'I cannot pretend to say anything, but speaking in the interests of the public——'

Mr. Auberon Quin rose suddenly to his feet.

'If you'll excuse me, gentlemen,' he said, 'I will step out for a moment into the air.'

'I'm so sorry, Auberon,' said Lambert, good-naturedly; 'do you feel bad?'

'Not bad exactly,' said Auberon, with self-restraint; 'rather good, if anything. Strangely and richly good. The fact is I want to reflect a little on those beautiful words that have just been uttered. "Speaking", yes, that was the phrase, "speaking in the interests of the public." One cannot get the honey from such things without being alone for a little.'

'Is he really off his chump, do you think?' asked Lambert.

The old President looked after him with queerly vigilant eyes.

'He is a man, I think,' he said, 'who cares for nothing but a joke. He is a dangerous man.'

Lambert laughed in the act of lifting some macaroni to his mouth.

'Dangerous!' he said. 'You don't know little Quin, sir!'

'Every man is dangerous,' said the old man without moving, 'who cares only for one thing. I was once dangerous myself.'

And with a pleasant smile he finished his coffee and rose, bowing profoundly, passed out into the fog, which had again grown dense and sombre. Three days afterwards they heard that he had died quietly in lodgings in Soho.

· · · · · ·

Drowned somewhere else in the dark sea of fog was a little figure shaking and quaking, with what might at first sight have seemed terror or ague: but which was really that strange malady, a lonely laughter. He was repeating over and over to himself with a rich accent—'But speaking in the interests of the public. . . .'

The Hill of Humour

'IN a little square garden of yellow roses, beside the sea,' said Auberon Quin, 'there was a Nonconformist minister who had never been to Wimbledon. His family did not understand his sorrow or the strange look in his eyes. But one day they repented their neglect, for they heard that a body had been found on the shore, battered, but wearing patent leather boots. As it happened, it turned out not to be the minister at all. But in the dead man's pocket there was a return ticket to Maidstone.'

There was a short pause as Quin and his friends Barker and Lambert went swinging on through the slushy grass of Kensington Gardens. Then Auberon resumed.

'That story,' he said reverently, 'is the test of humour.'

They walked on further and faster, wading through higher grass as they began to climb a slope.

'I perceive,' continued Auberon, 'that you have passed the test, and consider the anecdote excruciatingly funny; since you say nothing. Only coarse humour is received with pot-house applause. The great anecdote is received in silence, like a benediction. You felt pretty benedicted, didn't you, Barker?'

'I saw the point,' said Barker, somewhat loftily.

'Do you know,' said Quin, with a sort of idiot gaiety, 'I have lots of stories as good as that. Listen to this one.'

And he slightly cleared his throat.

'Dr. Polycarp was, as you all know, an unusually sallow

bimetallist. "There," people of wide experience would say, "There goes the sallowest bimetallist in Cheshire." Once this was said so that he overheard it: it was said by an actuary, under a sunset of mauve and grey. Polycarp turned upon him. "Sallow!" he cried fiercely, "sallow! *Quis tulerit Gracchos de seditione querentes.*" It was said that no actuary ever made game of Dr. Polycarp again.'

Barker nodded with a simple sagacity. Lambert only grunted.

'Here is another,' continued the insatiable Quin. 'In a hollow of the grey-green hills of rainy Ireland, lived an old, old woman, whose uncle was always Cambridge at the Boat Race. But in her grey-green hollows, she knew nothing of this: she didn't know that there was a Boat Race. Also she did not know that she had an uncle. She had heard of nobody at all, except of George the First, of whom she had heard (I know not why), and in whose historical memory she put her simple trust. And by and by, in God's good time, it was discovered that this uncle of hers was not really her uncle, and they came and told her so. She smiled through her tears, and said only, "Virtue is its own reward." '

Again there was a silence, and then Lambert said—

'It seems a bit mysterious.'

'Mysterious!' cried the other. 'The true humour is mysterious. Do you not realise the chief incident of the nineteenth and twentieth centuries?'

'And what's that?' asked Lambert, shortly.

'It is very simple,' replied the other. 'Hitherto it was the ruin of a joke that people did not see it. Now it is the sublime victory of a joke that people do not see it. Humour, my friends, is the one sanctity remaining to mankind. It is the one thing you are thoroughly afraid of. Look at that tree.'

His interlocutors looked vaguely towards a beech that leant out towards them from the ridge of the hill.

'If,' said Mr. Quin, 'I were to say that you did not see the great truths of science exhibited by that tree, though they stared any man of intellect in the face, what would you think or say? You would merely regard me as a pedant with some unimportant theory about vegetable cells. If I were to say that you did not see in that tree the vile misman-agement of local politics, you would dismiss me as a Socialist crank with some particular fad about public parks. If I were to say that you were guilty of the supreme blas-phemy of looking at that tree and not seeing in it a new religion, a special revelation of God, you would simply say I was a mystic, and think no more about me. But if'—and he lifted a portifical hand—'if I say that you cannot see the humour of that tree, and that I see the humour of it—my God! you will roll about at my feet.'

He paused a moment, and then resumed.

'Yes; a sense of humour, a weird and delicate sense of humour, is the new religion of mankind! It is towards that men will strain themselves with the asceticism of saints. Exercises, spiritual exercises, will be set in it. It will be asked, "Can you see the humour of this iron railing?" or "Can you see the humour of this field of corn? Can you see the humour of the stars? Can you see the humour of the sunsets?" How often I have laughed myself to sleep over a violet sunset.'

'Quite so,' said Mr. Barker, with an intelligent embar-rassment.

'Let me tell you another story. How often it happens

that the M.P.'s for Essex are less punctual than one would suppose. The least punctual Essex M.P., perhaps, was James Wilson, who said, in the very act of plucking a poppy——'

Lambert suddenly faced round and struck his stick into the ground in a defiant attitude.

'Auberon,' he said, 'chuck it. I won't stand it. It's all bosh.'

Both men stared at him, for there was something very explosive about the words, as if they had been corked up painfully for a long time.

'You have,' began Quin, 'no——'

'I don't care a curse,' said Lambert, violently, 'whether I have "a delicate sense of humour" or not. I won't stand it. It's all a confounded fraud. There's no joke in those infernal tales at all. You know there isn't as well as I do.'

'Well,' replied Quin, slowly, 'it is true that I, with my rather gradual mental processes, did not see any joke in them. But the finer sense of Barker perceived it.'

Barker turned a fierce red, but continued to stare at the horizon.

'You ass,' said Lambert; 'why can't you be like other people? Why can't you say something really funny, or hold your tongue? The man who sits on his hat in a pantomime is a long sight funnier than you are.'

Quin regarded him steadily. They had reached the top of the ridge and the wind struck their faces.

'Lambert,' said Auberon, 'you are a great and good man, though I'm hanged if you look it. You are more. You are a great revolutionist or deliverer of the world, and I look forward to seeing you carved in marble between Luther and Danton, if possible in your present attitude, the hat slightly on one side. I said as I came up the hill that the new

humour was the last of the religions. You have made it
the last of the superstitions. But let me give you a very
serious warning. Be careful how you ask me to do anything *outré,* to imitate the man in the pantomime, and to
sit on my hat. Because I am a man whose soul has been
emptied of all pleasures but folly. And for twopence I'd
do it.'

'Do it then,' said Lambert, swinging his stick impatiently. 'It would be funnier than the bosh you and Barker
talk.'

Quin, standing on the top of the hill, stretched his hand
out towards the main avenue of Kensington Gardens.

'Two hundred yards away,' he said, 'are all your fashionable acquaintances with nothing on earth to do but to stare
at each other and at us. We are standing upon an elevation
under the open sky, a peak as it were of fantasy, a Sinai of
humour. We are in a great pulpit or platform, lit up with
sunlight, and half London can see us. Be careful how you
suggest things to me. For there is in me a madness which
goes beyond martyrdom, the madness of an utterly idle
man.'

'I don't know what you are talking about,' said Lambert,
contemptuously. 'I only know I'd rather you stood on
your silly head, than talked so much.'

'Auberon! for goodness' sake. . . .' cried Barker, springing forward; but he was too late. Faces from all the benches
and avenues were turned in their direction. Groups stopped
and small crowds collected; and the sharp sunlight picked
out the whole scene in blue, green and black, like a picture
in a child's toy-book. And on the top of the small hill Mr.
Auberon Quin stood with considerable athletic neatness
upon his head, and waved his patent-leather boots in the air.

'For God's sake, Quin, get up, and don't be an idiot,' cried Barker, wringing his hands; 'we shall have the whole town here.'

'Yes, get up, get up, man,' said Lambert, amused and annoyed. 'I was only fooling; get up.'

Auberon did so with a bound, and flinging his hat higher than the trees, proceeded to hop about on one leg with a serious expression. Barker stamped wildly.

'Oh, let's get home, Barker, and leave him,' said Lambert; 'some of your proper and correct police will look after him. Here they come!'

Two grave-looking men in quiet uniforms came up the hill towards them. One held a paper in his hand.

'There he is, officer,' said Lambert, cheerfully: 'we ain't responsible for him.'

The officer looked at the capering Mr. Quin with a quiet eye.

'We have not come, gentlemen,' he said, 'about what I think you are alluding to. We have come from headquarters to announce the selection of His Majesty the King. It is the rule, inherited from the old *régime*, that the news should be brought to the new Sovereign immediately, wherever he is; so we have followed you across Kensington Gardens.'

Barker's eyes were blazing in his pale face. He was consumed with ambition throughout his life. With a certain dull magnanimity of the intellect he had really believed in the chance method of selecting despots. But this sudden suggestion, that the selection might have fallen upon him, unnerved him with pleasure.

'Which of us,' he began, and the respectful official interrupted him.

'Not you, sir, I am sorry to say. If I may be permitted to say so, we know your services to the Government, and should be very thankful if it were. The choice has fallen. . . .'

'God bless my soul!' said Lambert, jumping back two paces. 'Not me. Don't say I'm autocrat of all the Russias.'

'No, sir,' said the officer, with a slight cough and a glance towards Auberon, who was at that moment putting his head between his legs and making a noise like a cow; 'the gentleman whom we have to congratulate seems at the moment—er—er—occupied.'

'Not Quin!' shrieked Barker, rushing up to him; 'it can't be. Auberon, for God's sake pull yourself together. You've been made King!'

With his head still upside down between his legs, Mr. Quin answered modestly—

'I am not worthy. I cannot reasonably claim to equal the great men who have previously swayed the sceptre of Britain. Perhaps the only peculiarity that I can claim is that I am probably the first monarch that ever spoke out his soul to the people of England with his head and body in this position. This may in some sense give me, to quote a poem that I wrote in my youth—

> "A nobler office on the earth
> Than valour, power of brain, or birth
> Could give the warrior kings of old."

The intellect clarified by this posture——'

Lambert and Barker made a kind of rush at him.

'Don't you understand?' cried Lambert. 'It's not a joke. They've really made you King. By gosh! they must have rum taste.'

'The great Bishops of the Middle Ages,' said Quin, kicking his legs in the air, as he was dragged up more or less upside down, 'were in the habit of refusing the honour of election three times and then accepting it. A mere matter of detail separates me from those great men. I will accept the post three times and refuse it afterwards. Oh! I will toil for you, my faithful people! You shall have a banquet of humour.'

By this time he had been landed the right way up, and the two men were still trying in vain to impress him with the gravity of the situation.

'Did you not tell me, Wilfrid Lambert,' he said, 'that I should be of more public value if I adopted a more popular form of humour? And when should a popular form of humour be more firmly riveted upon me than now, when I have become the darling of a whole people? Officer,' he continued, addressing the startled messenger, 'are there no ceremonies to celebrate my entry into the city?'

'Ceremonies,' began the official, with embarrassment, 'have been more or less neglected for some little time, and——'

Auberon Quin began gradually to take off his coat.

'All ceremony,' he said, 'consists in the reversal of the obvious. Thus men, when they wish to be priests or judges, dress up like women. Kindly help me on with this coat.' And he held it out.

'But, your Majesty,' said the officer, after a moment's bewilderment and manipulation, 'you're putting it on with the tails in front.'

'The reversal of the obvious,' said the King, calmly, 'is as near as we can come to ritual with our imperfect apparatus. Lead on.'

The rest of that afternoon and evening was to Barker and Lambert a nightmare, which they could not properly realise or recall. The King, with his coat on the wrong way, went towards the streets that were awaiting him, and the old Kensington Palace which was the Royal residence. As he passed small groups of men, the groups turned into crowds, and gave forth sounds which seemed strange in welcoming an autocrat. Barker walked behind, his brain reeling, and, as the crowds grew thicker and thicker, the sounds became more and more unusual. And when he had reached the great market-place opposite the church, Barker knew that he had reached it, though he was roods behind, because a cry went up such as had never before greeted any of the kings of the earth.

BOOK TWO

*

CHAPTER I

The Charter of the Cities

LAMBERT was standing bewildered outside the door of the King's apartments amid the scurry of astonishment and ridicule. He was just passing out into the street, in a dazed manner, when James Barker dashed by him.

'Where are you going?' he asked.

'To stop all this foolery, of course,' replied Barker; and he disappeared into the room.

He entered it headlong, slamming the door, and slapping his incomparable silk hat on the table. His mouth opened, but before he could speak, the King said—

'Your hat, if you please.'

Fidgeting with his fingers, and scarcely knowing what he was doing, the young politician held it out.

The King placed it on his own chair, and sat on it.

'A quaint old custom,' he explained, smiling above the ruins. 'When the King receives the representative of the House of Barker, the hat of the latter is immediately destroyed in this manner. It represents the absolute finality of the act of homage expressed in the removal of it. It declares that never until that hat shall once more appear upon your head (a contingency which I firmly believe to be remote) shall the House of Barker rebel against the Crown of England.'

Barker stood with clenched fist, and shaking lip.

'Your jokes,' he began, 'and my property——' and then exploded with an oath, and stopped again.

'Continue, continue,' said the King, waving his hands.

'What does it all mean?' cried the other, with a gesture of passionate rationality. 'Are you mad?'

'Not in the least,' replied the King, pleasantly. 'Madmen are always serious; they go mad from lack of humour. You are looking serious yourself, James.'

'Why can't you keep it to your own private life?' expostulated the other. 'You've got plenty of money, and plenty of houses now to play the fool in, but in the interests of the public——'

'Epigrammatic,' said the King, shaking his finger sadly at him. 'None of your daring scintillations here. As to why I don't do it in private, I rather fail to understand your question. The answer is of comparative limpidity. I don't do it in private, because it is funnier to do it in public. You appear to think that it would be amusing to be dignified in the banquet hall and in the street, and at my own fireside (I could procure a fireside) to keep the company in a roar. But that is what every one does. Every one is grave in public, and funny in private. My sense of humour suggests the reversal of this; it suggests that one should be funny in public, and solemn in private. I desire to make the State functions, parliaments, coronations, and so on, one roaring old-fashioned pantomime. But, on the other hand, I shut myself up alone in a small store-room for two hours a day, where I am so dignified that I come out quite ill.'

By this time Barker was walking up and down the room, his frock-coat flapping like the black wings of a bird.

'Well, you will ruin the country, that's all,' he said.

'It seems to me,' said Auberon, 'that the tradition of ten centuries is being broken, and the House of Barker is rebelling against the Crown of England. It would be with regret (for I admire your appearance) that I should be obliged forcibly to decorate your head with the remains of this hat, but——'

'What I can't understand,' said Barker, flinging up his fingers with a feverish American movement, 'is why you don't care about anything else but your games.'

The King stopped sharply in the act of lifting the silken remnants, dropped them, and walked up to Barker, looking at him steadily.

'I made a kind of vow,' he said, 'that I would not talk seriously, which always means answering silly questions. But the strong man will always be gentle with politicians.

> "The shape my scornful looks deride
>   Required a God to form;"

if I may so theologically express myself. And for some reason I cannot in the least understand, I feel impelled to answer that question of yours, and to answer it as if there were really such a thing in the world as a serious subject. You ask me why I don't care for anything else. Can you tell me, in the name of all the gods you don't believe in, why I should care for anything else?'

'Don't you realise common public necessities?' cried Barker. 'Is it possible that a man of your intelligence does not know that it is every one's interest——'

'Don't you believe in Zoroaster? Is it possible that you neglect Mumbo-Jumbo?' returned the King, with startling animation. 'Does a man of your intelligence come to me with these damned early Victorian ethics? If, on studying my features and manner, you detect any particular resemblance to the Prince Consort, I assure you you are mistaken. Did Herbert Spencer ever convince you—did he ever convince anybody—did he ever for one mad moment convince himself—that it must be to the interest of the individual to feel a public spirit? Do you believe that, if you rule your department badly, you stand any more chance, or one half of the chance, of being guillotined, than an angler stands, of being pulled into the river by a strong pike? Herbert Spencer refrained from theft for the same reason that he refrained from wearing feathers in his hair, because he was an English gentleman with different tastes. I am an English gentleman with different tastes. He liked philosophy. I like art. He liked writing ten books on the nature of human society. I like to see the Lord Chamberlain walking in front of me with a piece of paper pinned to his coat-tails. It is my humour. Are you answered? At any rate, I have said my last serious word to-day, and my last serious word I trust for the remainder of my life in this Paradise of Fools. The remainder of my conversation with you to-day, which I trust will be long and stimulating, I propose to conduct in a new language of my own by means of rapid and symbolic movements of the left leg.' And he began to pirouette slowly round the room with a preoccupied expression.

Barker ran round the room after him, bombarding him with demands and entreaties. But he received no response except in the new language. He came out banging the door again, and sick like a man coming on shore. As he strode along the streets he found himself suddenly opposite Cicconani's restaurant, and for some reason there rose up before him the green fantastic figure of the Spanish General,

standing, as he had seen him last, at the door with the words
on his lips, 'You cannot argue with the choice of the soul.'

The King came out from his dancing with the air of a
man of business legitimately tired. He put on an overcoat,
lit a cigar, and went out into the purple night.

'I will go,' he said, 'and mingle with the people.'

He passed swiftly up a street in the neighbourhood of
Notting Hill, when suddenly he felt a hard object driven
into his waistcoat. He paused, put up a single eye-glass, and
beheld a boy with a wooden sword and a paper cocked hat,
wearing that expression of awed satisfaction with which a
child contemplates his work when he has hit some one very
hard. The King gazed thoughtfully for some time at his
assailant, and slowly took a note-book from his breast-
pocket.

'I have a few notes,' he said, 'for my dying speech;' and
he turned over the leaves. 'Dying speech for political
assassination; ditto, if by former friend—h'm, h'm. Dying
speech for death at hands of injured husband (repentant).
Dying speech for same (cynical). I am not quite sure
which meets the present. . . .'

'I'm the King of the Castle,' said the boy, truculently,
and very pleased with nothing in particular.

The King was a kind-hearted man, and very fond of
children, like all people who are fond of the ridiculous.

'Infant,' he said, 'I'm glad you are so stalwart a defender
of your old inviolate Notting Hill. Look up nightly to
that peak, my child, where it lifts itself among the stars so
ancient, so lonely, so unutterably Notting. So long as you
are ready to die for the sacred mountain, even if it were
ringed with all the armies of Bayswater——'

The King stopped suddenly, and his eyes shone.

'Perhaps,' he said, 'perhaps the noblest of all my conceptions. A revival of the arrogance of the old mediæval cities applied to our glorious suburbs. Clapham with a city guard. Wimbledon with a city wall. Surbiton tolling a bell to raise its citizens. West Hampstead going into battle with its own banner. It shall be done. I, the King, have said it.' And hastily presenting the boy with half-a-crown, remarking, 'For the war-chest of Notting Hill,' he ran violently home at such a rate of speed that crowds followed him for miles. On reaching his study, he ordered a cup of coffee, and plunged into profound meditation upon the project. At length he called his favourite Equerry, Captain Bowler, for whom he had a deep affection, founded principally upon the shape of his whiskers.

'Bowler,' he said, 'isn't there some society of historical research, or something of which I am an honorary member?'

'Yes, sir,' said Captain Bowler, rubbing his nose,' you are a member of "The Encouragers of Egyptian Renaissance," and "The Teutonic Tombs Club," and "The Society for the Recovery of London Antiquities," and——'

'That is admirable,' said the King. 'The London Antiquities does my trick. Go to the Society for the Recovery of London Antiquities and speak to their secretary, and their sub-secretary, and their president, and their vice-president, saying, "The King of England is proud, but the honorary member of the Society for the Recovery of London Antiquities is prouder than kings. I should like to tell you of certain discoveries I have made touching the neglected traditions of the London boroughs. The revelations may cause some excitement, stirring burning memories and touching old wounds in Shepherd's Bush and

Bayswater, in Pimlico and South Kensington. The King hesitates, but the honorary member is firm. I approach you invoking the vows of my initiation, the Sacred Seven Cats, the Poker of Perfection, and the Ordeal of the Indescribable Instant (forgive me if I mix up with the Clan-na-Gael or some other club I belong to), and ask you to permit me to read a paper at your next meeting on the 'Wars of the London Boroughs.'" Say all this to the Society, Bowler. Remember it very carefully, for it is most important, and I have forgotten it altogether, and send me another cup of coffee and some of the cigars that we keep for vulgar and successful people. I am going to write my paper.'

The Society for the Recovery of London Antiquities met a month after in a corrugated iron hall on the outskirts of one of the southern suburbs of London. A large number of people had collected there under the coarse and flaring gas-jets when the King arrived, perspiring and genial. On taking off his great-coat, he was perceived to be in evening dress, wearing the Garter. His appearance at the small table, adorned only with a glass of water, was received with respectful cheering.

The chairman (Mr. Huggins) said that he was sure that they had all been pleased to listen to such distinguished lecturers as they had heard for some time past (hear, hear). Mr. Burton (hear, hear), Mr. Cambridge, Professor King (loud and continued cheers), our old friend Peter Jessop, Sir William White (loud laughter), and other eminent men, had done honour to their little venture (cheers). But there were other circumstances which lent a certain unique quality to the present occasion (hear, hear). So far as his recollection went, and in connection with the Society for the Recovery of London Antiquities it went very far (loud cheers), he did not remember that any of their lecturers had borne the title of King. He would therefore call upon King Auberon briefly to address the meeting.

The King began by saying that this speech might be regarded as the first declaration of his new policy for the nation. 'At this supreme hour of my life I feel that to no one but the members of the Society for the Recovery of London Antiquities can I open my heart (cheers). If the world turns upon my policy, and the storms of popular hostility begin to rise (no, no), I feel that it is here, with my brave Recoverers around me, that I can best meet them, sword in hand' (loud cheers).

His Majesty then went on to explain that, now old age was creeping upon him, he proposed to devote his remaining strength to bringing about a keener sense of local patriotism in the various municipalities of London. How few of them knew the legends of their own boroughs! How many there were who had never heard of the true origin of the Wink of Wandsworth! What a large proportion of the younger generation in Chelsea neglected to perform the old Chelsea Chuff! Pimlico no longer pumped the Pimlies. Battersea had forgotten the name of Blick.

There was a short silence, and then a voice said 'Shame.'

The King continued: 'Being called, however unworthily, to this high estate, I have resolved that, so far as possible, this neglect shall cease. I desire no military glory. I lay claim to no constitutional equality with Justinian or Alfred. If I can go down to history as the man who saved from extinction a few old English customs, if our descendants can say it was through this man, humble as he was, that the Ten Turnips are still eaten in Fulham, and the Putney parish councillor still shaves one half of his head, I shall look my great fathers reverently but not fearfully in the face when I go down to the last house of Kings.'

The King paused, visibly affected, but collecting himself, resumed once more.

'I trust that to very few of you, at least, I need dwell on the sublime origins of these legends. The very names of your boroughs bear witness to them. So long as Hammersmith is called Hammersmith, its people will live in the shadow of that primal hero, the Blacksmith, who led the democracy of the Broadway into battle till he drove the chivalry of Kensington before him and overthrew them at that place which in honour of the best blood of the defeated aristocracy is still called Kensington Gore. Men of Hammersmith will not fail to remember that the very name of Kensington originated from the lips of their hero. For at the great banquet of reconciliation held after the war, when the disdainful oligarchs declined to join in the songs of the men of the Broadway (which are to this day of a rude and popular character), the great Republican leader, with his rough humour, said the words which are written in gold upon his monument, "Little birds that can sing and won't sing, must be made to sing." So that the Eastern Knights were called Cansings or Kensings ever afterwards. But you also have great memories, O men of Kensington! You showed that you could sing, and sing great war-songs. Even after the dark day of Kensington Gore, history will not forget those three Knights who guarded your disordered retreat from Hyde Park (so called from your hiding there), those three Knights after whom Knightsbridge is named. Nor will it forget the day of your reemergence, purged in the fire of calamity, cleansed of your oligarchic corruptions, when, sword in hand, you drove the Empire of Hammersmith back mile by mile, swept it past its own Broadway, and broke it at last in a battle so long and bloody that the birds of prey have left their name upon it. Men have called it, with austere irony, the Ravenscourt. I shall not, I trust, wound the patriotism of Bayswater, or the lonelier pride of Brompton, or that of any other historic township, by taking these two special examples. I select them, not because they are more glorious than the rest, but partly from personal association (I am myself descended from one of the three heroes of Knightsbridge), and partly from the consciousness that I am an amateur antiquarian, and cannot presume to deal with times and places more remote and more mysterious. It is not for me to settle the question between two such men as Professor Hugg and Sir William Whisky as to whether Notting Hill means Nutting Hill (in allusion to the rich woods which no longer cover it), or whether it is a corruption of Nothing-ill, referring to its reputation among the ancients as an Earthly Paradise. When a Podkins and a Jossy confess themselves doubtful about the boundaries of West Kensington (said to have been traced in the blood of Oxen), I need not be ashamed to confess a similar doubt. I will ask you to excuse me from further history, and to assist me with your encouragement in dealing with the problem which faces us to-day. Is this ancient spirit of the London townships to die out? Are our omnibus conductors and policemen to lose altogether that light which we see so often in their eyes, the dreamy light of

> "Old unhappy far-off things
> And battles long ago"

—to quote the words of a little-known poet who was a

friend of my youth? I have resolved, as I have said, so far
as possible, to preserve the eyes of policemen and omnibus
conductors in their present dreamy state. For what is a
state without dreams? And the remedy I propose is as
follows:

'To-morrow morning at twenty-five minutes past ten,
if Heaven spares my life, I purpose to issue a Proclamation.
It has been the work of my life, and is about half finished.
With the assistance of a whisky and soda, I shall conclude
the other half to-night, and my people will receive it to-
morrow. All these boroughs where you were born, and
hope to lay your bones, shall be reinstated in their ancient
magnificence—Hammersmith, Kensington, Bayswater,
Chelsea, Battersea, Clapham, Balham, and a hundred
others. Each shall immediately build a city wall with gates
to be closed at sunset. Each shall have a city guard, armed
to the teeth. Each shall have a banner, a coat-of-arms, and,
if convenient, a gathering cry. I will not enter into the
details now, my heart is too full. They will be found in
the proclamation itself. You will all, however, be subject
to enrolment in the local city guards, to be summoned together by a thing called the Tocsin, the meaning of which
I am studying in my researches into history. Personally, I
believe a tocsin to be some kind of highly paid official. If,
therefore, any of you happen to have such a thing as a
halberd in the house, I should advise you to practise with it
in the garden.'

Here the King buried his face in his handkerchief and
hurriedly left the platform, overcome by emotions.

The members of the Society for the Recovery of London
Antiquities rose in an indescribable state of vagueness.
Some were purple with indignation: an intellectual few

were purple with laughter; the great majority found their minds a blank. There remains a tradition that one pale face with burning blue eyes remained fixed upon the lecturer, and after the lecture a red-haired boy ran out of the room.

CHAPTER II

The Council of the Provosts

THE King got up early next morning and came down three
steps at a time like a schoolboy. Having eaten his breakfast
hurriedly, but with an appetite, he summoned one of the
highest officials of the Palace, and presented him with a
shilling. 'Go and buy me,' he said, 'a shilling paint-box,
which you will get, unless the mists of time mislead me, in
a shop at the corner of the second and dirtier street that
leads out of Rochester Row. I have already requested the
Master of the Buckhounds to provide me with cardboard.
It seemed to me (I know not why) that it fell within his
department.'

The King was happy all that morning with his cardboard and his paint-box. He was engaged in designing the
uniforms and coats-of-arms for the various municipalities
of London. They gave him deep and no inconsiderable
thought. He felt the responsibility.

'I cannot think,' he said, 'why people should think the
names of places in the country more poetical than those in
London. Shallow romanticists go away in trains and stop
in places called Hugmy-in-the-Hole, or Bumps-on-the-
Puddle. And all the time they could, if they liked, go and
live at a place with the dim, divine name of St. John's
Wood. I have never been to St. John's Wood. I dare
not. I should be afraid of the innumerable night of fir
trees, afraid to come upon a blood-red cup and the beat-
ing of the wings of the Eagle. But all these things can

be imagined by remaining reverently in the Harrow train.'

And he thoughtfully retouched his design for the head-dress of the halberdier of St. John's Wood, a design in black and red, compounded of a pine tree and the plumage of an eagle. Then he turned to another card. 'Let us think of milder matters,' he said. 'Lavender Hill! Could any of your glebes and combes and all the rest of it produce so fragrant an Idea? Think of a mountain of lavender lifting itself in purple poignancy into the silver skies and filling men's nostrils with a new breath of life—a purple hill of incense. It is true that upon my few excursions of discovery on a halfpenny tram I have failed to hit the precise spot. But it must be there; some poet called it by its name. There is at least warrant enough for the solemn purple plumes (following the botanical formation of lavender) which I have required people to wear in the neighbourhood of Clapham Junction. It is so everywhere, after all. I have never been actually to Southfields, but I suppose a scheme of lemons and olives represent their austral instincts. I have never visited Parson's Green, or seen either the Green or the Parson, but surely the pale-green shovel-hats I have designed must be more or less in the spirit. I must work in the dark and let my instincts guide me. The great love I bear to my people will certainly save me from distressing their noble spirit or violating their great traditions.'

As he was reflecting in this vein, the door was flung open, and an official announced Mr. Barker and Mr. Lambert.

Mr. Barker and Mr. Lambert were not particularly surprised to find the King sitting on the floor amid a litter of water-colour sketches. They were not particularly surprised because the last time they had called on him they had found him sitting on the floor, surrounded by a litter of children's bricks, and the time before surrounded by a litter of wholly unsuccessful attempts to make paper darts. But the trend of the royal infant's remarks, uttered from amid this infantile chaos, was not quite the same affair. For some time they let him babble on, conscious that his remarks meant nothing. And then a horrible thought began to steal over the mind of James Barker. He began to think that the King's remarks did not mean nothing.

'In God's name, Auberon,' he suddenly volleyed out, startling the quiet hall, 'you don't mean that you are really going to have these city guards and city walls and things?'

'I am indeed,' said the infant, in a quiet voice. 'Why shouldn't I have them? I have modelled them precisely on your political principles. Do you know what I've done, Barker? I've behaved like a true Barkerian. I've . . . but perhaps it won't interest you, the account of my Barkerian conduct.'

'Oh, go on, go on,' cried Barker.

'The account of my Barkerian conduct,' said Auberon, calmly, 'seems not only to interest, but to alarm you. Yet it is very simple. It merely consists in choosing all the provosts under any new scheme by the same principle by which you have caused the central despot to be appointed. Each provost, of each city, under my charter, is to be appointed by rotation. Sleep, therefore, my Barker, a rosy sleep.'

Barker's wild eyes flared.

'But in God's name, don't you see, Quin, that the thing is quite different? In the centre it doesn't matter so much, just because the whole object of despotism is to get some sort of unity. But if any damned parish can go to any damned man——'

'I see your difficulty,' said King Auberon, calmly. 'You feel that your talents may be neglected. Listen!' And he rose with immense magnificence. 'I solemnly give to my liege subject, James Barker, my special and splendid favour, the right to override the obvious text of the Charter of the Cities, and to be, in his own right, Lord High Provost of South Kensington. And now, my dear James, you are all right. Good day.'

'But——' began Barker.

'The audience is at an end, Provost,' said the King, smiling.

How far his confidence was justified, it would require a somewhat complicated description to explain. 'The Great Proclamation of the Charter of the Free Cities' appeared in due course that morning, and was posted by bill-stickers all over the front of the Palace, the King assisting them with animated directions, and standing in the middle of the road, with his head on one side, contemplating the result. It was also carried up and down the main thoroughfares by sandwichmen, and the King was, with difficulty, restrained from going out in that capacity himself, being, in fact, found by the Groom of the Stole and Captain Bowler, struggling between two boards. His excitement had positively to be quieted like that of a child.

The reception which the Charter of the Cities met at the hands of the public may mildly be described as mixed. In one sense it was popular enough. In many happy homes that remarkable legal document was read aloud on winter evenings amid uproarious appreciation, when everything had been learnt by heart from that quaint but immortal old classic, Mr. W. W. Jacobs. But, when it was discovered that the King had every intention of seriously requiring the provisions to be carried out, of insisting that the grotesque cities, with their tocsins and city guards, should really come into existence, things were thrown into a far angrier confusion. Londoners had no particular objection to the King making a fool of himself, but they became indignant when it became evident that he wished to make fools of them; and protests began to come in.

The Lord High Provost of the Good and Valiant City of West Kensington wrote a respectful letter to the King, explaining that upon State occasions it would, of course, be his duty to observe what formalities the King thought proper, but that it was really awkward for a decent householder not to be allowed to go out and put a post-card in a pillar-box without being escorted by five heralds, who announced with formal cries and blasts of a trumpet, that the Lord High Provost desired to catch the post.

The Lord High Provost of North Kensington, who was a prosperous draper, wrote a curt business note, like a man complaining of a railway company, stating that definite inconvenience had been caused him by the presence of the halberdiers, whom he had to take with him everywhere. When attempting to catch an omnibus to the City, he had found that while room could have been found for himself, the halberdiers had a difficulty in getting into the vehicle— believe him, theirs faithfully.

The Lord High Provost of Shepherd's Bush said his wife did not like men hanging round the kitchen.

The King was always delighted to listen to these grievances, delivering lenient and kingly answers, but as he always insisted, as the absolute *sine qua non*, that verbal complaints should be presented to him with the fullest pomp of trumpets, plumes, and halberds, only a few resolute spirits were prepared to run the gauntlet of the little boys in the street.

Among these, however, was prominent the abrupt and business-like gentleman who ruled North Kensington. And he had before long, occasion to interview the King about a matter wider and even more urgent than the problem of the halberdiers and the omnibus. This was the greatest question which then and for long afterwards brought a stir to the blood and a flush to the cheek of all the speculative builders and house agents from Shepherd's Bush to the Marble Arch, and from Westbourne Grove to High Street, Kensington. I refer to the great affair of the improvements in Notting Hill. The scheme was conducted chiefly by Mr. Buck, the abrupt North Kensington magnate, and by Mr. Wilson, the Provost of Bayswater. A great thoroughfare was to be driven through three boroughs, through West Kensington, North Kensington and Notting Hill, opening at one end into Hammersmith Broadway, and at the other into Westbourne Grove. The negotiations, buyings, sellings, bullying and bribing took ten years, and by the end of it Buck, who had conducted them almost single-handed, had proved himself a man of the strongest type of material energy and material diplomacy. And just as his splendid patience and more splendid impatience had finally brought him victory, when workmen were already demolishing houses and walls along the great line from Hammersmith, a sudden obstacle appeared that had neither been reckoned with nor dreamed of, a small and strange obstacle, which, like a speck of grit in a great machine, jarred the whole vast scheme and brought it to a standstill, and Mr. Buck, the draper, getting with great impatience into his robes of office and summoning with indescribable disgust his halberdiers, hurried over to speak to the King.

Ten years had not tired the King of his joke. There were still new faces to be seen looking out from the symbolic head-gears he had designed, gazing at him from amid the pastoral ribbons of Shepherd's Bush or from under the sombre hoods of the Blackfriars Road. And the interview which was promised him with the Provost of North Kensington he anticipated with a particular pleasure, for 'he never really enjoyed,' he said, 'the full richness of the mediæval garments unless the people compelled to wear them were very angry and business-like.'

Mr. Buck was both. At the King's command the door of the audience-chamber was thrown open and a herald appeared in the purple colours of Mr. Buck's commonwealth emblazoned with the Great Eagle which the King had attributed to North Kensington, in vague reminiscence of Russia, for he always insisted on regarding North Kensington as some kind of semi-arctic neighbourhood. The herald announced that the Provost of that city desired audience of the King.

'From North Kensington?' said the King, rising graciously. 'What news does he bring from that land of high hills and fair women? He is welcome.'

The herald advanced into the room, and was immediately followed by twelve guards clad in purple, who were followed by an attendant bearing the banner of the Eagle, who was followed by another attendant bearing the keys of the city upon a cushion, who was followed by Mr. Buck in a great hurry. When the King saw his strong animal face and steady eyes, he knew that he was in the presence of a great man of business, and consciously braced himself.

'Well, well,' he said, cheerily coming down two or three steps from a daïs, and striking his hands lightly together, 'I am glad to see you. Never mind, never mind. Ceremony is not everything.'

'I don't understand your Majesty,' said the Provost, stolidly.

'Never mind, never mind,' said the King, gaily. 'A knowledge of Courts is by no means an unmixed merit; you will do it next time, no doubt.'

The man of business looked at him sulkily from under his black brows and said again without show of civility—

'I don't follow you.'

'Well, well,' replied the King, good-naturedly, 'if you ask me I don't mind telling you, not because I myself attach any importance to these forms in comparison with the Honest Heart. But it is usual—it is usual—that is all, for a man when entering the presence of Royalty to lie down on his back on the floor and elevating his feet towards heaven (as the source of Royal power) to say three times "Monarchical institutions improve the manners." But there, there—such pomp is far less truly dignified than your simple kindliness.'

The Provost's face was red with anger and he maintained silence.

'And now,' said the King, lightly, and with the exasperating air of a man softening a snub; 'what delightful weather we are having! You must find your official robes warm, my Lord. I designed them for your own snow-bound land.'

'They're as hot as hell,' said Buck, briefly. 'I came here on business.'

'Right,' said the King, nodding a great number of times with quite unmeaning solemnity; 'right, right, right. Business, as the sad glad old Persian said, is business. Be punctual. Rise early. Point the pen to the shoulder. Point the pen to the shoulder, for you know not whence you come nor why. Point the pen to the shoulder, for you know not when you go nor where.'

The Provost pulled a number of papers from his pocket and savagely flapped them open.

'Your Majesty may have heard,' he began, sarcastically, 'of Hammersmith and a thing called a road. We have been at work ten years buying property and getting compulsory powers and fixing compensation and squaring vested interests, and now at the very end, the thing is stopped by a fool. Old Prout, who was Provost of Notting Hill, was a business man, and we dealt with him quite satisfactorily. But he's dead, and the cursed lot has fallen to a young man named Wayne, who's up to some game that's perfectly incomprehensible to me. We offer him a better price than any one ever dreamt of, but he won't let the road go through. And his Council seem to be backing him up. It's midsummer madness.'

The King, who was rather inattentively engaged in drawing the Provost's nose with his finger on the window-pane, heard the last two words.

'What a perfect phrase that is,' he said. ' "Midsummer madness!" '

'The chief point is,' continued Buck, doggedly, 'that the only part that is really in question is one dirty little street—Pump Street—a street with nothing in it but a public house and a penny toy-shop, and that sort of thing. All the respectable people of Notting Hill have accepted our compensation. But the ineffable Wayne sticks out over Pump Street. Says he's Provost of Notting Hill. He's only Provost of Pump Street.'

'A good thought,' replied Auberon. 'I like the idea of a Provost of Pump Street. Why not let him alone?'

'And drop the whole scheme!' cried out Buck, with a burst of brutal spirit. 'I'll be damned if we do. No. I'm for sending in workmen to pull down without more ado.'

'Strike for the purple Eagle,' cried the King, hot with historical associations.

'I'll tell you what it is,' said Buck, losing his temper altogether. 'If your Majesty would spend less time in insulting respectable people with your silly coats-of-arms, and more time over the business of the nation——'

The King's brow wrinkled thoughtfully.

'The situation is not bad,' he said; 'the haughty burgher defying the King in his own Palace. The burgher's head should be thrown back and the right arm extended; the left may be lifted towards Heaven, but that I leave to your private religious sentiment. I have sunk back in this chair, stricken with baffled fury. Now again, please.'

Buck's mouth opened like a dog's, but before he could speak another herald appeared at the door.

'The Lord High Provost of Bayswater,' he said, 'desires an audience.'

'Admit him,' said Auberon. 'This *is* a jolly day.'

The halberdiers of Bayswater wore a prevailing uniform of green, and the banner which was borne after them was emblazoned with a green bay-wreath on a silver ground, which the King, in the course of his researches into a bottle of champagne, had discovered to be the quaint old punning cognisance of the city of Bayswater.

C

'It is a fit symbol,' said the King, 'your immortal bay-wreath. Fulham may seek for wealth, and Kensington for art, but when did the men of Bayswater care for anything but glory?'

Immediately behind the banner, and almost completely hidden by it, came the Provost of the city, clad in splendid robes of green and silver with white fur and crowned with bay. He was an anxious little man with red whiskers, originally the owner of a small sweet-stuff shop.

'Our cousin of Bayswater,' said the King, with delight; 'what can we get for you?' The King was heard also distinctly to mutter, 'Cold beef, cold 'am, cold chicken,' his voice dying into silence.

'I came to see your Majesty,' said the Provost of Bayswater, whose name was Wilson, 'about that Pump Street affair.'

'I have just been explaining the situation to his Majesty,' said Buck, curtly, but recovering his civility. 'I am not sure, however, whether his Majesty knows how much the matter affects you also.'

'It affects both of us, yer see, yer Majesty, as this scheme was started for the benefit of the 'ole neighbourhood. So Mr. Buck and me we put our 'eads together——'

The King clasped his hands.

'Perfect,' he cried in ecstasy. 'Your heads together! I can see it! Can't you do it now? Oh, do do it now.'

A smothered sound of amusement appeared to come from the halberdiers, but Mr. Wilson looked merely bewildered, and Mr. Buck merely diabolical.

'I suppose,' he began, bitterly, but the King stopped him with a gesture of listening.

'Hush,' he said, 'I think I hear some one else coming. I seem to hear another herald, a herald whose boots creak.'

As he spoke another voice cried from the doorway—
'The Lord High Provost of South Kensington desires an audience.'

'The Lord High Provost of South Kensington!' cried the King. 'Why, that is my old friend James Barker! What does he want, I wonder? If the tender memories of friendship have not grown misty, I fancy he wants something for himself, probably money. How are you, James?'

Mr. James Barker, whose guard was attired in a splendid blue, and whose blue banner bore three gold birds singing, rushed, in his blue and gold robes, into the room. Despite the absurdity of all the dresses, it was worth noticing that he carried his better than the rest, though he loathed it as much as any of them. He was a gentleman, and a very handsome man, and could not help unconsciously wearing even his preposterous robe as it should be worn. He spoke quickly, but with the slight initial hesitation he always showed in addressing the King, due to suppressing an impulse to address his old acquaintance in the old way.

'Your Majesty—pray forgive my intrusion. It is about this man at Pump Street. I see you have Buck here, so you have probably heard what is necessary. I——'

The King swept his eyes anxiously round the room, which now blazed with the trappings of three cities.

'There is one thing necessary,' he said.

'Yes, your Majesty,' said Mr. Wilson of Bayswater, a little eagerly. 'What does yer Majesty think necessary?'

'A little yellow,' said the King, firmly. 'Send for the Provost of West Kensington.'

Amid some materialistic protests he was sent for, and

arrived with his yellow halberdiers in his saffron robes, wiping his forehead with a handkerchief. After all, placed as he was, he had a good deal to say on the matter.

'Welcome, West Kensington,' said the King. 'I have long wished to see you, touching that matter of the Hammersmith land to the south of the Rowton House. Will you hold it feudally from the Provost of Hammersmith? You have only to do him homage by putting his left arm in his overcoat and then marching home in state.'

'No, your Majesty; I'd rather not,' said the Provost of West Kensington, who was a pale young man with a fair moustache and whiskers, who kept a successful dairy.

The King struck him heartily on the shoulder.

'The fierce old West Kensington blood,' he said; 'they are not wise who ask it to do homage.'

Then he glanced again round the room. It was full of a roaring sunset of colour, and he enjoyed the sight, possible to so few artists—the sight of his own dreams moving and blazing before him. In the foreground the yellow of the West Kensington liveries outlined itself against the dark blue draperies of South Kensington. The crests of these again brightened suddenly into green as the almost woodland colours of Bayswater rose behind them. And over and behind all, the great purple plumes of North Kensington showed almost funereal and black.

'There is something lacking,' said the King, 'something lacking. What can—Ah, there it is!—there it is!'

In the doorway had appeared a new figure, a herald in flaming red. He cried in a loud but unemotional voice—

'The Lord High Provost of Notting Hill desires an audience.'

Enter a Lunatic

THE King of the Fairies, who was, it is to be presumed, the godfather of King Auberon, must have been very favourable on this particular day to his fantastic godchild, for with the entrance of the guard of the Provost of Notting Hill there was a certain more or less inexplicable addition to his delight. The wretched navvies and sandwich-men who carried the colours of Bayswater or South Kensington, engaged merely for the day to satisfy the Royal hobby, slouched into the room with a comparatively hang-dog air, and a great part of the King's intellectual pleasure consisted in the contrast between the arrogance of their swords and feathers and the meek misery of their faces. But these Notting Hill halberdiers in their red tunics belted with gold had the air rather of an absurd gravity. They seemed, so to speak, to be taking part in the joke. They marched and wheeled into position with an almost startling dignity and discipline.

They carried a yellow banner with a great red lion, named by the King as the Notting Hill emblem, after a small public-house in the neighbourhood, which he once frequented.

Between the two lines of his followers there advanced towards the King a tall, red-haired young man, with high features, and bold blue eyes. He would have been called handsome, but that a certain indefinable air of his nose being too big for his face, and his feet for his legs, gave him a look of awkwardness and extreme youth. His robes were red, according to the King's heraldry, and alone among the Provosts, he was girt with a great sword. This was Adam Wayne, the intractable Provost of Notting Hill.

The King flung himself back in his chair, and rubbed his hands.

'What a day, what a day!' he said to himself. 'Now there'll be a row. I'd no idea it would be such fun as it is. These Provosts are so very indignant, so very reasonable, so very right. This fellow, by the look in his eyes, is even more indignant than the rest. No sign in those large blue eyes, at any rate, of ever having heard of a joke. He'll remonstrate with the others, and they'll remonstrate with him, and they'll all make themselves sumptuously happy remonstrating with me.'

'Welcome, my Lord,' he said aloud. 'What news from the Hill of a Hundred Legends? What have you for the ear of your King? I know that troubles have arisen between you and these others, our cousins, but these troubles it shall be our pride to compose. And I doubt not, and cannot doubt, that your love for me is not less tender, no less ardent than theirs.'

Mr. Buck made a bitter face, and James Barker's nostrils curled; Wilson began to giggle faintly, and the Provost of West Kensington followed in a smothered way. But the big blue eyes of Adam Wayne never changed, and he called out in an odd, boyish voice down the hall—

'I bring homage to my King. I bring him the only thing I have—my sword.'

And with a great gesture he flung it down on the ground, and knelt on one knee behind it.

There was a dead silence.

'I beg your pardon,' said the King, blankly.

'You speak well, sire,' said Adam Wayne, 'as you ever speak, when you say that my love is not less than the love of these. Small would it be if it were not more. For I am heir of your scheme—the child of the great Charter. I stand here for the rights the Charter gave me, and I swear, by your sacred crown, that where I stand, I stand fast.'

The eyes of all five men stood out of their heads.

Then Buck said, in his jolly, jarring voice: 'Is the whole world mad?'

The King sprang to his feet, and his eyes blazed.

'Yes,' he cried, in a voice of exultation, 'the whole world is mad, but Adam Wayne and me. It is true as death what I told you long ago, James Barker, seriousness sends men mad. You are mad, because you care for politics, as mad as a man who collects tram tickets. Buck is mad, because he cares for money, as mad as a man who lives on opium. Wilson is mad, because he thinks himself right, as mad as a man who thinks himself God Almighty. The Provost of West Kensington is mad, because he thinks he is respectable, as mad as a man who thinks he is a chicken. All men are mad, but the humourist, who cares for nothing and possesses everything. I thought that there was only one humourist in England. Fools!—dolts!—open your cows' eyes; there are two! In Notting Hill—in that unpromising elevation—there has been born an artist! You thought to spoil my joke, and bully me out of it, by becoming more and more modern, more and more practical, more and more bustling and rational. Oh, what a feast it was to answer you by becoming more and more august, more and more gracious, more and more ancient and mellow! But this lad has seen how to bowl me out. He has answered me

back, vaunt for vaunt, rhetoric for rhetoric. He has lifted
the only shield I cannot break, the shield of an impenetrable
pomposity. Listen to him. You have come, my Lord,
about Pump Street?'

'About the city of Notting Hill,' answered Wayne,
proudly. 'Of which Pump Street is a living and rejoicing
part.'

'Not a very large part,' said Barker, contemptuously.

'That which is large enough for the rich to covet,' said
Wayne, drawing up his head, 'is large enough for the poor
to defend.'

The King slapped both his legs, and waved his feet for a
second in the air.

'Every respectable person in Notting Hill,' cut in Buck,
with his cold, coarse voice, 'is for us and against you. I
have plenty of friends in Notting Hill.'

'Your friends are those who have taken your gold for
other men's hearthstones, my Lord Buck,' said Provost
Wayne. 'I can well believe they are your friends.'

'They've never sold dirty toys, anyhow,' said Buck,
laughing shortly.

'They've sold dirtier things,' said Wayne, calmly; 'they
have sold themselves.'

'It's no good, my Buckling,' said the King, rolling about
on his chair. 'You can't cope with this chivalrous elo-
quence. You can't cope with an artist. You can't cope
with the humourist of Notting Hill. O, *Nunc dimittis*—
that I have lived to see this day! Provost Wayne, you stand
firm?'

'Let them wait and see,' said Wayne. 'If I stood firm
before, do you think I shall weaken now that I have seen
the face of the King? For I fight for something greater, if

greater there can be, than the hearthstones of my people and the Lordship of the Lion. I fight for your royal vision, for the great dream you dreamt of the League of the Free Cities. You have given me this liberty. If I had been a beggar and you had flung me a coin, if I had been a peasant in a dance and you had flung me a favour, do you think I would have let it be taken by any ruffians on the road? This leadership and liberty of Notting Hill is a gift from your Majesty. And if it is taken from me, by God! it shall be taken in battle, and the noise of that battle shall be heard in the flats of Chelsea and in the studios of St. John's Wood.'

'It is too much—it is too much,' said the King. 'Nature is weak. I must speak to you, brother artist, without further disguise. Let me ask you a solemn question. Adam Wayne, Lord High Provost of Notting Hill, don't you think it splendid?'

'Splendid!' cried Adam Wayne. 'It has the splendour of God.'

'Bowled out again,' said the King. 'You will keep up the pose. Funnily, of course, it is serious. But seriously, isn't it funny?'

'What?' asked Wayne, with the eyes of a baby.

'Hang it all, don't play any more. The whole business—the Charter of the Cities. Isn't it immense?'

'Immense is no unworthy word for that glorious design.'

'Oh, hang you—but, of course, I see. You want me to clear the room of these reasonable sows. You want the two humourists alone together. Leave us, gentlemen.'

Buck threw a sour look at Barker, and at a sullen signal the whole pageant of blue and green, of red, gold and

c*

purple rolled out of the room, leaving only two in the great hall, the King sitting in his seat on the daïs, and the red-clad figure still kneeling on the floor before his fallen sword.

The King bounded down the steps and smacked Provost Wayne on the back.

'Before the stars were made,' he cried, 'we were made for each other. It is too beautiful. Think of the valiant independence of Pump Street. That is the real thing. It is the deification of the ludicrous.'

The kneeling figure sprang to his feet with a fierce stagger.

'Ludicrous!' he cried, with a fiery face.

'Oh come, come,' said the King, impatiently. 'You needn't keep it up with me. The augurs must wink sometimes from sheer fatigue of the eyelids. Let us enjoy this for half an hour, not as actors, but as dramatic critics. Isn't it a joke?'

Adam Wayne looked down like a boy, and answered in a constrained voice—

'I do not understand your Majesty. I cannot believe that while I fight for your royal charter your Majesty deserts me for these dogs of the gold hunt.'

'Oh, damn your—— But what's this? What the devil's this?'

The King stared into the young Provost's face, and in the twilight of the room began to see that his face was quite white and his lip shaking.

'What in God's name is the matter?' cried Auberon, holding his wrist.

Wayne flung back his face, and the tears were shining on it.

'I am only a boy,' he said, 'but it's true. I would paint the Red Lion on my shield if I had only my blood.'

King Auberon dropped the hand and stood without stirring, thunderstruck.

'My God in Heaven!' he said; 'is it possible that there is within the four seas of Britain a man who takes Notting Hill seriously——?'

'And my God in Heaven!' said Wayne passionately; 'is it possible that there is within the four seas of Britain a man who does not take it seriously?'

The King said nothing, but merely went back up the steps of the daïs, like a man dazed. He fell back in his chair again and kicked his heels.

'If this sort of thing is to go on,' he said weakly, 'I shall begin to doubt the superiority of art to life. In Heaven's name, do not play with me. Do you really mean that you are—God help me!—a Notting Hill patriot—that you are——'

Wayne made a violent gesture, and the King soothed him wildly.

'All right—all right—I see you are; but let me take it in. You do really propose to fight these modern improvers with their boards and inspectors and surveyors and all the rest of it——'

'Are they so terrible?' asked Wayne, scornfully.

The King continued to stare at him as if he were a human curiosity.

'And I suppose,' he said, 'that you think that the dentists and small tradesmen and maiden ladies who inhabit Notting Hill, will rally with war-hymns to your standard?'

'If they have blood they will,' said the Provost.

'And I suppose,' said the King, with his head back among

the cushions, 'that it never crossed your mind that'—his voice seemed to lose itself luxuriantly—'never crossed your mind that any one ever thought that the idea of a Notting Hill idealism was—er—slightly—slightly ridiculous.'

'Of course they think so,' said Wayne. 'What was the meaning of mocking the prophets?'

'Where?' asked the King, leaning forward. 'Where in Heaven's name did you get this miraculously inane idea?'

'You have been my tutor, Sire,' said the Provost, 'in all that is high and honourable.'

'Eh?' said the King.

'It was your Majesty who first stirred my dim patriotism into flame. Ten years ago, when I was a boy (I am only nineteen), I was playing on the slope of Pump Street, with a wooden sword and a paper helmet, dreaming of great wars. In an angry trance I struck out with my sword and stood petrified, for I saw that I had struck you, Sire, my King, as you wandered in a noble secrecy, watching over your people's welfare. But I need have had no fear. Then was I taught to understand Kingliness. You neither shrank nor frowned. You summoned no guards. You invoked no punishments. But in august and burning words, which are written in my soul, never to be erased, you told me ever to turn my sword against the enemies of my inviolate city. Like a priest pointing to the altar, you pointed to the hill of Notting. "So long," you said, "as you are ready to die for the sacred mountain, even if it were ringed with all the armies of Bayswater." I have not forgotten the words, and I have reason now to remember them, for the hour is come and the crown of your prophecy. The sacred hill is ringed with the armies of Bayswater, and I am ready to die.'

The King was lying back in his chair, a kind of wreck.

'O Lord, Lord, Lord,' he murmured, 'what a life! what a life! All my work! I seem to have done it all. So you're the red-haired boy that hit me in the waistcoat. What have I done? God, what have I done? I thought I would have a joke, and I have created a passion. I tried to compose a burlesque, and it seems to be turning halfway through into an epic. What is to be done with such a world? In the Lord's name, wasn't the joke broad and bold enough? I abandoned my subtle humour to amuse you, and I seem to have brought tears to your eyes. What's to be done with people when you write a pantomime for them—call the sausages classic festoons, and the policeman cut in two a tragedy of public duty? But why am I talking? Why am I asking questions of a nice young gentleman who is totally mad? What is the good of it? What is the good of anything? O Lord, O Lord!'

Suddenly he pulled himself upright.

'Don't you really think the sacred Notting Hill at all absurd?'

'Absurd?' asked Wayne blankly. 'Why should I?'

The King stared back equally blankly.

'I beg your pardon?' he said.

'Notting Hill,' said the Provost, simply, 'is a rise or high ground of the common earth, on which men have built houses to live, in which they are born, fall in love, pray, marry, and die. Why should I think it absurd?'

The King smiled.

'Because, my Leonidas——' he began, then suddenly, he knew not how, found his mind was a total blank. After all, why was it absurd? Why was it absurd? He felt as if the floor of his mind had given way. He felt as all men feel when their first principles are hit hard with a question.

Barker always felt so when the King said, 'Why trouble about politics?'

The King's thoughts were in a kind of rout; he could not collect them.

'It is generally felt to be a little funny,' he said, vaguely.

'I suppose,' said Adam, turning on him with a fierce suddenness, 'I suppose you fancy crucifixion was a serious affair?'

'Well, I——' began Auberon, 'I admit I have generally thought it had its graver side.'

'Then you are wrong,' said Wayne, with incredible violence. 'Crucifixion is comic. It is exquisitely diverting. It was an absurd and obscene kind of impaling reserved for people who were made to be laughed at—for slaves and provincials—for dentists and small tradesmen, as you would say. I have seen the grotesque gallows-shape, which the little Roman gutter-boys scribbled on walls as a vulgar joke, blazing on the pinnacles of the temples of the world. And shall I turn back?'

The King made no answer.

Adam went on, his voice ringing in the roof.

'This laughter with which men tyrannise is not the great power you think it. Peter was crucified, and crucified head downwards. What could be funnier than the idea of a respectable old Apostle upside down? What could be more in the style of your modern humour? But what was the good of it? Upside down or right side up, Peter was Peter to mankind. Upside down he still hangs over Europe, and millions move and breathe only in the life of his church.'

King Auberon got up absently.

'There is something in what you say,' he said. 'You seem to have been thinking, young man.'

'Only feeling, sire,' answered the Provost. 'I was born, like other men, in a spot of the earth which I loved because I had played boys' games there, and fallen in love, and talked with my friends through nights that were nights of the gods. And I feel the riddle. These little gardens where we told our loves. These streets where we brought out our dead. Why should they be commonplace? Why should they be absurd? Why should it be grotesque to say that a pillar-box is poetic when for a year I could not see a red pillar-box against the yellow evening in a certain street without being wracked with something of which God keeps the secret, but which is stronger than sorrow or joy? Why should any one be able to raise a laugh by saying "the Cause of Notting Hill"?—Notting Hill where thousands of immortal spirits blaze with alternate hope and fear.'

Auberon was flicking dust off his sleeve with quite a new seriousness on his face, distinct from the owlish solemnity which was the pose of his humour.

'It is very difficult,' he said at last. 'It is a damned difficult thing. I see what you mean—I agree with you even up to a point—or I should like to agree with you, if I were young enough to be a prophet and poet. I feel a truth in everything you say until you come to the words "Notting Hill." And then I regret to say that the old Adam awakes roaring with laughter and makes short work of the new Adam, whose name is Wayne.'

For the first time Provost Wayne was silent, and stood gazing dreamily at the floor. Evening was closing in, and the room had grown darker.

'I know,' he said, in a strange, almost sleepy voice, 'there is truth in what you say, too. It is hard not to laugh at the common names—I only say we should not. I have thought of a remedy; but such thoughts are rather terrible.'

'What thoughts?' asked Auberon.

The Provost of Notting Hill seemed to have fallen into a kind of trance; in his eyes was an elvish light.

'I know of a magic wand, but it is a wand that only one or two may rightly use, and only seldom. It is a fairy wand of great fear, stronger than those who use it—often frightful, often wicked to use. But whatever is touched with it is never again wholly common. Whatever is touched with it takes a magic from outside the world. If I touch, with this fairy wand, the railways and the roads of Notting Hill, men will love them, and be afraid of them for ever.'

'What the devil are you talking about?' asked the King.

'It has made mean landscapes magnificent, and hovels outlast cathedrals,' went on the madman. 'Why should it not make lamp-posts fairer than Greek lamps, and an omnibus ride like a painted ship? The touch of it is the finger of a strange perfection.'

'What is your wand?' cried the King, impatiently.

'There it is,' said Wayne; and pointed to the floor, where his sword lay flat and shining.

'The sword !' cried the King; and sprang up straight on the daïs.

'Yes, yes,' cried Wayne, hoarsely. 'The things touched by that are not vulgar. The things touched by that——'

King Auberon made a gesture of horror.

'You will shed blood for that!' he cried. 'For a cursed point of view——'

'Oh, you kings, you kings,' cried out Adam, in a burst of scorn. 'How humane you are, how tender, how con-

siderate. You will make war for a frontier, or the imports
of a foreign harbour; you will shed blood for the precise
duty on lace, or the salute to an admiral. But for the things
that make life itself worthy or miserable—how humane you
are. I say here, and I know well what I speak of, there were
never any necessary wars but the religious wars. There
were never any just wars but the religious wars. There
were never any humane wars but the religious wars. For
these men were fighting for something that claimed, at
least, to be the happiness of a man, the virtue of a man. A
Crusader thought, at least, that Islam hurt the soul of every
man, king or tinker, that it could really capture. I think
Buck and Barker and these rich vultures hurt the soul of
every man, hurt every inch of the ground, hurt every brick
of the houses, that they can really capture. Do you think I
have no right to fight for Notting Hill, you whose English
Government has so often fought for tomfooleries? If, as
your rich friends say, there are no gods, and the skies are
dark above us, what should a man fight for, but the place
where he had the Eden of childhood and the short heaven
of first love? If no temples and no scriptures are sacred,
what is sacred if a man's own youth is not sacred?'

The King walked a little restlessly up and down the daïs.

'It is hard,' he said, biting his lips, 'to assent to a view so
desperate—so responsible. . . .'

As he spoke, the door of the audience chamber fell ajar,
and through the aperture came, like the sudden chatter of
a bird, the high, nasal, but well-bred voice of Barker.

'I said to him quite plainly—the public interests——'

Auberon turned on Wayne with violence.

'What the devil is all this? What am I saying? What
are you saying? Have you hypnotised me? Curse your

uncanny blue eyes! Let me go. Give me back my sense of humour. Give it me back. Give it me back, I say!'

'I solemnly assure you,' said Wayne uneasily, with a gesture, as if feeling all over himself, 'that I haven't got it.'

The King fell back in his chair, and went into a roar of Rabelaisian laughter.

'I don't think you have,' he cried.

BOOK THREE

★

CHAPTER I

The Mental Condition of
Adam Wayne

A LITTLE while after the King's accession a small book of
poems appeared, called 'Hymns on the Hill.' They were
not good poems, nor was the book successful, but it
attracted a certain amount of attention from one particular
school of critics. The King himself, who was a member of
the school, reviewed it in his capacity as literary critic to
'Straight from the Stables,' a sporting journal. They were
known as the Hammock School, because it had been cal-
culated malignantly by an enemy that no less than thirteen
of their delicate criticisms had begun with the words, 'I
read this book in a hammock: half asleep in the sleepy sunlight, I. . . .'; after that there were important differences.
Under these conditions they liked everything, but especially
everything silly. 'Next to authentic goodness in a book,'
they said—'next to authentic goodness in a book (and that,
alas! we never find) we desire a rich badness.' Thus it
happened that their praise (as indicating the presence of a
rich badness) was not universally sought after, and authors
became a little disquieted when they found the eye of the
Hammock School fixed upon them with peculiar favour.

The peculiarity of 'Hymns on the Hill' was the celebra-
tion of the poetry of London as distinct from the poetry of
the country. This sentiment or affectation was, of course,
not uncommon in the twentieth century, nor was it, al-

thoughsometimesexaggerated, andsometimesartificial, by
any means without a great truth at its root, for there is one
respect in which a town must be more poetical than the
country, since it is closer to the spirit of man; for London,
if it be not one of the masterpieces of man, is at least one of
his sins. A street is really more poetical than a meadow,
because a street has a secret. A street is going somewhere,
and a meadow nowhere. But, in the case of the book
called 'Hymns on the Hill,' there was another peculiarity,
which the King pointed out with great acumen in his
review. He was naturally interested in the matter, for he
had himself published a volume of lyrics about London
under his pseudonym of 'Daisy Daydream.'

This difference, as the King pointed out, consisted in
the fact that, while mere artificers like 'Daisy Daydream'
(on whose elaborate style the King, over his signature of
'Thunderbolt,' was perhaps somewhat too severe) thought
to praise London by comparing it to the country—using
nature, that is, as a background from which all poetical
images had to be drawn—the more robust author of
'Hymns on the Hill' praised the country, or nature, by
comparing it to the town, and used the town itself as a
background. 'Take,' said the critic, 'the typically feminine
lines, "To the Inventor of The Hansom Cab"'—

> "Poet, whose cunning carved this amorous shell,
>   Where twain may dwell."

'Surely,' wrote the King, 'no one but a woman could
have written those lines. A woman has always a weakness
for nature; with her, art is only beautiful as an echo or
shadow of it. She is praising the hansom cab by theme and
theory, but her soul is still a child by the sea, picking up

shells. She can never be utterly of the town, as a man can; indeed, do we not speak (with sacred propriety) of "a man about town"? Who ever spoke of a woman about town? However much, physically, "about town" a woman may be, she still models herself on nature; she tries to carry nature with her; she bids grasses to grow on her head, and furry beasts to bite her about the throat. In the heart of a dim city, she models her hat on a flaring cottage garden of flowers. We, with our nobler civic sentiment, model ours on a chimney pot; the ensign of civilisation. And rather than be without birds, she will commit massacre, that she may turn her head into a tree, with dead birds to sing on it.'

This kind of thing went on for several pages, and then the critic remembered his subject, and returned to it.

> ' Poet, whose cunning carved this amorous shell,
> Where twain may dwell.'

'The peculiarity of these fine though feminine lines,' continued 'Thunderbolt,' 'is, as we have said, that they praise the hansom cab by comparing it to the shell, to a natural thing. Now, hear the author of "Hymns of the Hill," and how he deals with the same subject. In his fine nocturne, entitled "The Last Omnibus," he relieves the rich and poignant melancholy of the theme by a sudden sense of rushing at the end—

> "The wind round the old street corner
> Swung sudden and quick as a cab."

'Here the distinction is obvious. "Daisy Daydream" thinks it a great compliment to a hansom cab to be compared to one of the spiral chambers of the sea. And the author of "Hymns on the Hill" thinks it a great compli-

ment to the immortal whirlwind to be compared to a
hackney coach. He surely is the real admirer of London.
We have no space to speak of all his perfect applications of
the idea; of the poem in which, for instance, a lady's eyes
are compared, not to stars, but to two perfect street-lamps
guiding the wanderer. We have no space to speak of the
fine lyric, recalling the Elizabethan spirit, in which the poet,
instead of saying that the rose and the lily contend in her
complexion, says, with a purer modernism, that the red
omnibus of Hammersmith and the white omnibus of Fulham fight there for the mastery. How perfect the image of
two contending omnibuses!'

Here, somewhat abruptly, the review concluded, probably because the King had to send off his copy at that
moment, as he was in some want of money. But the King
was a very good critic, whatever he may have been as
King, and he had, to a considerable extent, hit the right
nail on the head. 'Hymns on the Hill' was not at all like
the poems originally published in praise of the poetry of
London. And the reason was that it was really written by
a man who had seen nothing else but London, and who
regarded it, therefore, as the universe. It was written by a
raw, red-headed lad of seventeen, named Adam Wayne,
who had been born in Notting Hill. An accident in his
seventh year prevented his being taken away to the seaside,
and thus his whole life had been passed in his own Pump
Street, and in its neighbourhood. And the consequence
was, that he saw the street-lamps as things quite as eternal
as the stars; the two fires were mingled. He saw the houses
as things enduring, like the mountains, and so he wrote
about them as one would write about mountains. Nature
puts on a disguise when she speaks to every man; to this

man she put on the disguise of Notting Hill. Nature would mean to a poet born in the Cumberland hills, a stormy sky-line and sudden rocks. Nature would mean to a poet born in the Essex flats, a waste of splendid waters and splendid sunsets. So nature meant to this man Wayne a line of violet roofs and lemon lamps, the chiaroscuro of the town. He did not think it clever or funny to praise the shadows and colours of the town; he had seen no other shadows or colours, and so he praised them—because they were shadows and colours. He saw all this because he was a poet, though in practice a bad poet. It is too often forgotten that just as a bad man is nevertheless a man, so a bad poet is nevertheless a poet.

Mr. Wayne's little volume of verse was a complete failure; and he submitted to the decision of fate with a quite rational humility, went back to his work, which was that of a draper's assistant, and wrote no more. He still retained his feeling about the town of Notting Hill, because he could not possibly have any other feeling, because it was the back and base of his brain. But he does not seem to have made any particular attempt to express it or insist upon it.

He was a genuine natural mystic, one of those who live on the border of fairyland. But he was perhaps the first to realise how often the boundary of fairyland runs through a crowded city. Twenty feet from him (for he was very short-sighted) the red and white and yellow suns of the gas-lights thronged and melted into each other like an orchard of fiery trees, the beginning of the woods of elf-land.

But, oddly enough, it was because he was a small poet that he came to his strange and isolated triumph. It was because he was a failure in literature that he became a portent in English history. He was one of those to whom nature has given the desire without the power of artistic expression. He had been a dumb poet from his cradle. He might have been so to his grave, and carried unuttered into the darkness a treasure of new and sensational song. But he was born under the lucky star of a single coincidence. He happened to be at the head of his dingy municipality at the time of the King's jest, at the time when all municipalities were suddenly commanded to break out into banners and flowers. Out of the long procession of the silent poets who have been passing since the beginning of the world, this one man found himself in the midst of an heraldic vision, in which he could act and speak and live lyrically. While the author and the victims alike treated the whole matter as a silly public charade, this one man, by taking it seriously, sprang suddenly into a throne of artistic omnipotence. Armour, music, standards, watch-fires, the noise of drums, all the theatrical properties were thrown before him. This one poor rhymester, having burnt his own rhymes, began to live that life of open air and acted poetry of which all the poets of the earth have dreamed in vain; the life for which the Iliad is only a cheap substitute.

Upwards from his abstracted childhood, Adam Wayne had grown strongly and silently in a certain quality or capacity which is in modern cities almost entirely artificial, but which can be natural, and was primarily almost brutally natural in him, the quality or capacity of patriotism. It exists, like other virtues and vices, in a certain undiluted reality. It is not confused with all kinds of other things. A child speaking of his country or his village may make every mistake in Mandeville or tell every lie in Munchausen, but in his statement there will be no psychological lies any more than there can be in a good song.

Adam Wayne, as a boy, had for his dull streets in Notting Hill the ultimate and ancient sentiment that went out to Athens or Jerusalem. He knew the secret of the passion, those secrets which make real old national songs sound so strange to our civilisation. He knew that real patriotism tends to sing about sorrows and forlorn hopes much more than about victory. He knew that in proper names themselves is half the poetry of all national poems. Above all, he knew the supreme psychological fact about patriotism, as certain in connection with it as that a fine shame comes to all lovers, the fact that the patriot never under any circumstances boasts of the largeness of his country, but always, and of necessity, boasts of the smallness of it.

All this he knew, not because he was a philosopher or a genius, but because he was a child. Any one who cares to walk up a side slum like Pump Street, can see a little Adam claiming to be king of a paving-stone. And he will always be proudest if the stone is almost too narrow for him to keep his feet inside it.

It was while he was in such a dream of defensive battle, marking out some strip of street or fortress of steps as the limit of his haughty claim, that the King had met him, and, with a few words flung in mockery, ratified for ever the strange boundaries of his soul. Thenceforward the fanciful idea of the defence of Notting Hill in war became to him a thing as solid as eating or drinking or lighting a pipe. He disposed his meals for it, altered his plans for it, lay awake in the night and went over it again. Two or three shops were to him an arsenal; an area was to him a moat; corners of balconies and turns of stone steps were points for the location of a culverin or an archer. It is almost impossible to convey to any ordinary imagination the degree to

which he had transmitted the leaden London landscape to
a romantic gold. The process began almost in babyhood,
and became habitual like a literal madness. It was felt most
keenly at night, when London is really herself, when her
lights shine in the dark like the eyes of innumerable cats,
and the outline of the dark houses has the bold simplicity
of blue hills. But for him the night revealed instead of
concealing, and he read all the blank hours of morning and
afternoon, by a contradictory phrase, in the light of that
darkness. To this man, at any rate, the inconceivable had
happened. The artificial city had become to him nature,
and he felt the curb-stones and gas-lamps as things as
ancient as the sky.

One instance may suffice. Walking along Pump Street
with a friend, he said, as he gazed dreamily at the iron fence
of a little front garden, 'How those railings stir one's
blood.'

His friend, who was also a great intellectual admirer,
looked at them painfully, but without any particular
emotion. He was so troubled about it that he went back
quite a large number of times on quiet evenings and stared
at the railings, waiting for something to happen to his
blood, but without success. At last he took refuge in asking
Wayne himself. He discovered that the ecstasy lay in the
one point he had never noticed about the railings even after
his six visits, the fact that they were like the great majority
of others in London, shaped at the top after the manner of
a spear. As a child, Wayne had half unconsciously compared them with the spears in pictures of Lancelot and St.
George, and had grown up under the shadow of the graphic
association. Now, whenever he looked at them, they were
simply the serried weapons that made a hedge of steel

round the sacred homes of Notting Hill. He could not have cleansed his mind of that meaning even if he tried. It was not a fanciful comparison, or anything like it. It would not have been true to say that the familiar railings reminded him of spears; it would have been far truer to say that the familiar spears occasionally reminded him of railings.

A couple of days after his interview with the King, Adam Wayne was pacing like a caged lion in front of five shops that occupied the upper end of the disputed street. They were a grocer's, a chemist's, a barber's, an old curiosity shop, and a toy-shop that sold also newspapers. It was these five shops which his childish fastidiousness had first selected as the essentials of the Notting Hill campaign, the citadel of the city. If Notting Hill was the heart of the universe, and Pump Street was the heart of Notting Hill, this was the heart of Pump Street. The fact that they were all small and side by side realised that feeling for a formidable comfort and compactness which, as we have said, was the heart of his patriotism and of all patriotism. The grocer (who had a wine and spirit licence) was included because he could provision the garrison; the old curiosity shop because it contained enough swords, pistols, partisans, cross-bows, and blunderbusses to arm a whole irregular regiment; the toy and paper shop because Wayne thought a free press an essential centre for the soul of Pump Street; the chemist's to cope with outbreaks of disease among the besieged; and the barber's because it was in the middle of all the rest, and the barber's son was an intimate friend and spiritual affinity.

It was a cloudless October evening settling down through purple into pure silver around the roofs and chimneys of the steep little street, which looked black and sharp and dramatic. In the deep shadows the gas-lit shop fronts

gleamed like five fires in a row, and before them, darkly
outlined like a ghost against some purgatorial furnaces,
passed to and fro the tall bird-like figure and eagle nose of
Adam Wayne.

He swung his stick restlessly, and seemed fitfully talking
to himself.

'There are, after all, enigmas,' he said, 'even to the man
who has faith. There are doubts that remain even after the
true philosophy is completed in every rung and rivet. And
here is one of them. Is the normal human need, the normal
human condition, higher or lower than those special states
of the soul which call out a doubtful and dangerous glory?
those special powers of knowledge or sacrifice which are
made possible only by the existence of evil? Which should
come first to our affections, the enduring sanities of peace
or the half-maniacal virtues of battle? Which should come
first, the man great in the daily round or the man great in
emergency? Which should come first, to return to the
enigma before me, the grocer or the chemist? Which is
more certainly the stay of the city, the swift chivalrous
chemist or the benignant all-providing grocer? In such
ultimate spiritual doubts it is only possible to choose a side
by the higher instincts and to abide the issue. In any case,
I have made my choice. May I be pardoned if I choose
wrongly, but I choose the grocer.'

'Good morning, sir,' said the grocer, who was a middle-
aged man, partially bald, with harsh red whiskers and
beard, and forehead lined with all the cares of the small
tradesman. 'What can I do for you, sir?'

Wayne removed his hat on entering the shop, with a
ceremonious gesture, which, slight as it was, made the
tradesman eye him with the beginnings of wonder.

'I come, sir,' he said soberly, 'to appeal to your patriotism.'

'Why, sir,' said the grocer, 'that sounds like the times when I was a boy and we used to have elections.'

'You will have them again,' said Wayne, firmly, 'and far greater things. Listen, Mr. Mead. I know the temptations which a grocer has to a too cosmopolitan philosophy. I can imagine what it must be to sit all day as you do surrounded with wares from all the ends of the earth, from strange seas that we have never sailed and strange forests that we could not even picture. No Eastern king ever had such argosies or such cargoes coming from the sunrise and the sunset, and Solomon in all his glory was not enriched like one of you. India is at your elbow,' he cried, lifting his voice and pointing his stick at a drawer of rice, the grocer making a movement of some alarm, 'China is before you, Demerara is behind you, America is above your head, and at this very moment, like some old Spanish admiral, you hold Tunis in your hands.'

Mr. Mead dropped the box of dates which he was just lifting, and then picked it up again vaguely.

Wayne went on with a heightened colour, but in a lowered voice.

'I know, I say, the temptations of so international, so universal a vision of wealth. I know that it must be your danger not to fall like many trasdesmen into too dusty and mechanical a narrowness, but rather to be too broad, to be too general, too liberal. If a narrow nationalism be the danger of the pastry-cook, who makes his own wares under his own heavens, no less is cosmopolitanism the danger of the grocer. But I come to you in the name of that patriotism which no wanderings or enlightenments should ever

wholly extinguish, and I ask you to remember Notting
Hill. For, after all, in this cosmopolitan magnificence, she
has played no small part. Your dates may come from the
tall palms of Barbary, your sugar from the strange islands
of the tropics, your tea from the secret villages of the
Empire of the Dragon. That this room might be furnished,
forests may have been spoiled under the Southern Cross,
and leviathans speared under the Polar Star. But you
yourself—surely no inconsiderable treasure—you yourself,
the brain that wields these vast interests—you yourself, at
least, have grown to strength and wisdom between these
grey houses and under this rainy sky. This city which made
you, and thus made your fortunes, is threatened with war.
Come forth and tell to the ends of the earth this lesson.
Oil is from the North and fruits from the South; rices are
from India and spices from Ceylon; sheep are from New
Zealand and men from Notting Hill.'

The grocer sat for some little while with dim eyes, and
his mouth open, looking rather like a fish. Then he
scratched the back of his head, and said nothing. Then he
said—

'Anything out of the shop, sir?'

Wayne looked round in a dazed way. Seeing a pile of
tins of pine-apple chunks, he waved his stick generally
towards them.

'Yes,' he said, 'I'll take those.'

'All those, sir?' said the grocer, with greatly increased
interest.

'Yes, yes; all those,' replied Wayne, still a little bewildered, like a man splashed with cold water.

'Very good, sir; thank you, sir,' said the grocer with
animation. 'You may count upon my patriotism, sir.'

'I count upon it already,' said Wayne, and passed out into the gathering night.

The grocer put the box of dates back in its place.

'What a nice fellow he is,' he said. 'It's odd how often they are nice. Much nicer than those as are all right.'

Meanwhile Adam Wayne stood outside the glowing chemist's shop, unmistakably wavering.

'What a weakness it is,' he muttered. 'I have never got rid of it from childhood. The fear of this magic shop. The grocer is rich, he is romantic, he is poetical in the truest sense, but he is not—no, he is not supernatural. But the chemist! All the other shops stand in Notting Hill, but this stands in Elf-land. Look at those great burning bowls of colour. It must be from them that God paints the sunsets. It is superhuman, and the superhuman is all the more uncanny when it is beneficent. That is the root of the fear of God. I am afraid. But I must be a man and enter.'

He was a man, and entered. A short, dark young man was behind the counter, with spectacles, and greeted him with a bright but entirely business-like smile.

'A fine evening, sir,' he said.

'Fine, indeed, strange Father,' said Adam, stretching his hands somewhat forward. 'It is on such clear and mellow nights that your shop is most itself. Then they appear most perfect, those moons of green and gold and crimson, which from afar, oft guide the pilgrim of pain and sickness to this house of merciful witchcraft.'

'Can I get you anything?' asked the chemist.

'Let me see,' said Wayne, in a friendly but vague manner. 'Let me have some Sal Volatile.'

'Eightpence, tenpence, or one and sixpence a bottle?' said the young man genially.

'One and six—one and six,' replied Wayne, with a wild submissiveness. 'I come to ask you, Mr. Bowles, a terrible question.'

He paused and collected himself.

'It is necessary,' he muttered—'it is necessary to be tactful, and to suit the appeal to each profession in turn.

'I come,' he resumed aloud, 'to ask you a question which goes to the roots of your miraculous toils. Mr. Bowles, shall all this witchery cease?' And he waved his stick around the shop.

Meeting with no answer, he continued with animation—

'In Notting Hill we have felt to its core the elfish mystery of your profession. And now Notting Hill itself is threatened.'

'Anything more, sir?' asked the chemist.

'Oh,' said Wayne, somewhat disturbed—'oh, what is it chemists sell? Quinine, I think. Thank you. Shall it be destroyed? I have met these men of Bayswater and North Kensington—Mr. Bowles, they are materialists. They see no witchery in your work, even when it is brought within their own borders. They think the chemist is commonplace. They think him human.'

The chemist appeared to pause, only a moment, to take in the insult, and immediately said—

'And the next article, please?'

'Alum,' said the Provost, wildly. 'I resume. It is in this sacred town alone that your priesthood is reverenced. Therefore, when you fight for us you fight not only for yourself, but for everything you typify. You fight not only for Notting Hill, but for Fairyland, for as surely as Buck and Barker and such men hold sway, the sense of Fairyland in some strange manner diminishes.'

'Anything more, sir?' asked Mr. Bowles, with unbroken cheerfulness.

'Oh yes, jujubes—Gregory powder—magnesia. The danger is imminent. In all this matter I have felt that I fought not merely for my own city (though to that I owe all my blood), but for all places in which these great ideas could prevail. I am fighting not merely for Notting Hill, but for Bayswater itself; for North Kensington itself. For if the gold-hunters prevail, these also will lose all their ancient sentiments and all the mystery of their national soul. I know I can count upon you.'

'Oh, yes, sir,' said the chemist, with great animation, 'we are always glad to oblige a good customer.'

Adam Wayne went out of the shop with a deep sense of fulfilment of soul.

'It is so fortunate,' he said, 'to have tact, to be able to play upon the peculiar talents and specialities, the cosmospolitanism of the grocer and the world-old necromancy of the chemist. Where should I be without tact?'

D

CHAPTER II

The Remarkable Mr. Turnbull

AFTER two more interviews with shopmen, however, the patriot's confidence in his own psychological diplomacy began vaguely to wane. Despite the care with which he considered the peculiar rationale and the peculiar glory of each separate shop, there seemed to be something unresponsive about the shopmen. Whether it was a dark resentment against the uninitiate for peeping into their masonic magnificence, he could not quite conjecture.

His conversation with the man who kept the shop of curiosities had begun encouragingly. The man who kept the shop of curiosities had indeed enchanted him with a phrase. He was standing drearily at the door of his shop, a wrinkled man with a grey pointed beard, evidently a gentleman who had come down in the world.

'And how does your commerce go, you strange guardian of the past?' said Wayne, affably.

'Well, sir, not very well,' replied the man, with that patient voice of his class which is one of the most heartbreaking things in the world. 'Things are terribly quiet.'

Wayne's eyes shone suddenly.

'A great saying,' he said, 'worthy of a man whose merchandise is human history. Terribly quiet; that is in two words the spirit of this age, as I have felt it from my cradle. I sometimes wondered how many other people felt the oppression of this union between quietude and terror. I see blank well-ordered streets and men in black moving about inoffensively, sullenly. It goes on day after day, day after day, and nothing happens; but to me it is like a dream from which I might wake screaming. To me the straightness of our life is the straightness of a thin cord stretched tight. Its stillness is terrible. It might snap with a noise like thunder. And you who sit, amid the *débris* of the great wars, you who sit, as it were, upon a battlefield, you know that war was less terrible than this evil peace; you know that the idle lads who carried those swords under Francis or Elizabeth, the rude Squire or Baron who swung that mace about in Picardy or Northumberland battles, may have been terribly noisy, but were not like us, terribly quiet.'

Whether it was a faint embarrassment of conscience as to the original source and date of the weapons referred to, or merely an engrained depression, the guardian of the past looked, if anything, a little more worried.

'But I do not think,' continued Wayne, 'that this horrible silence of modernity will last, though I think for the present it will increase. What a farce is this modern liberality. Freedom of speech means practically in our modern civilisation that we must only talk about unimportant things. We must not talk about religion, for that is illiberal; we must not talk about bread and cheese, for that is talking shop; we must not talk about death, for that is depressing; we must not talk about birth, for that is indelicate. It cannot last. Something must break this strange indifference, this strange dreamy egoism, this strange loneliness of millions in a crowd. Something must break it. Why should it not be you and I? Can you do nothing else but guard relics?'

The shopman wore a gradually clearing expression, which would have led those unsympathetic with the cause of the Red Lion to think that the last sentence was the only one to which he had attached any meaning.

'I am rather old to go into a new business,' he said, 'and I don't quite know what to be either.'

'Why not,' said Wayne, gently having reached the crisis of his delicate persuasion—'why not be a Colonel?'

It was at this point, in all probability, that the interview began to yield more disappointing results. The man appeared inclined at first to regard the suggestion of becoming a Colonel as outside the sphere of immediate and relevant discussion. A long exposition of the inevitable war of independence, coupled with the purchase of a doubtful sixteenth-century sword for an exaggerated price, seemed to resettle matters. Wayne left the shop, however, somewhat infected with the melancholy of its owner.

That melancholy was completed at the barber's.

'Shaving, sir?' inquired that artist from inside his shop.

'War!' replied Wayne, standing on the threshold.

'I beg your pardon,' said the other, sharply.

'War!' said Wayne, warmly. 'But not for anything inconsistent with the beautiful and the civilised arts. War for beauty. War for society. War for peace. A great chance is offered you of repelling that slander which, in defiance of the lives of so many artists, attributes poltoonery to those who beautify and polish the surface of our lives. Why should not hairdressers be heroes? Why should not——'

'Now, you get out,' said the barber, irascibly. 'We don't want any of your sort here. You get out.'

And he came forward with the desperate annoyance of a mild person when enraged.

Adam Wayne laid his hand for a moment on the sword, then dropped it.

'Notting Hill,' he said, 'will need her bolder sons;' and he turned gloomily to the toy-shop.

It was one of those queer little shops so constantly seen in the side streets of London, which must be called toy-shops only because toys upon the whole predominate; for the remainder of goods seem to consist of almost everything else in the world—tobacco, exercise-books, sweet-stuff, novelettes, halfpenny paper clips, halfpenny pencil sharpeners, bootlaces, and cheap fireworks. It also sold newspapers, and a row of dirty-looking posters hung along the front of it.

'I am afraid,' said Wayne, as he entered, 'that I am not getting on with these tradesmen as I should. Is it that I have neglected to rise to the full meaning of their work? Is there some secret buried in each of these shops which no mere poet can discover?'

He stepped to the counter with a depression which he rapidly conquered as he addressed the man on the other side of it—a man of short stature, and hair prematurely white, and the look of a large baby.

'Sir,' said Wayne, 'I am going from house to house in this street of ours, seeking to stir up some sense of the danger which now threatens our city. Nowhere have I felt my duty so difficult as here. For the toy-shop keeper has to do with all that remains to us of Eden before the first wars began. You sit here meditating continually upon the wants of that wonderful time when every staircase leads to the stars, and every garden-path to the other end of no-where. Is it thoughtlessly, do you think, that I strike the dark old drum of peril in the paradise of children? But consider a moment; do not condemn me hastily. Even that paradise itself contains the rumour or beginning of that danger, just as the Eden that was made for perfection contained the terrible tree. For judge childhood, even by your own arsenal of its pleasures. You keep bricks; you make yourself thus, doubtless, the witness of the constructive instinct older than the destructive. You keep dolls; you make yourself the priest of that divine idolatry. You keep Noah's Arks; you perpetuate the memory of the salvation of all life as a precious, an irreplaceable thing. But do you keep only, sir, the symbols of this prehistoric sanity, this childish rationality of the earth? Do you not keep more terrible things? What are those boxes, seemingly of lead soldiers, that I see in that glass case? Are they not witnesses to that terror and beauty, that desire for a lovely death, which could not be excluded even from the immortality of Eden? Do not despise the lead soldiers, Mr. Turnbull.'

'I don't,' said Mr. Turnbull, of the toy-shop, shortly, but with great emphasis.

'I am glad to hear it,' replied Wayne. 'I confess that I feared for my military schemes the awful innocence of your profession. How, I thought to myself, will this man, used only to the wooden swords that give pleasure, think of the steel swords that give pain? But I am at least partly reassured. Your tone suggests to me that I have at least the entry of a gate of your fairyland—the gate through which the soldiers enter, for it cannot be denied—I ought, sir, no longer to deny, that it is of soldiers that I come to speak. Let your gentle employment make you merciful towards the troubles of the world. Let your own silvery experience tone down our sanguine sorrows. For there is war in Notting Hill.'

The little toy-shop keeper sprang up suddenly, slapping his fat hands like two fans on the counter.

'War?' he cried. 'Not really, sir? Is it true? Oh, what
a joke! Oh, what a sight for sore eyes?'

Wayne was almost taken aback by this outburst.

'I am delighted,' he stammered. 'I had no notion——'

He sprang out of the way just in time to avoid Mr.
Turnbull, who took a flying leap over the counter and
dashed to the front of the shop.

'You look here, sir,' he said; 'you just look here.'

He came back with two of the torn posters in his hand
which were flapping outside his shop.

'Look at those, sir,' he said, and flung them down on the
counter.

Wayne bent over them, and read on one—

'LAST FIGHTING
REDUCTION OF THE CENTRAL DERVISH CITY
REMARKABLE, ETC.'

On the other he read—

'LAST SMALL REPUBLIC ANNEXED
NICARAGUAN CAPITAL SURRENDERS AFTER A
MONTH'S FIGHTING
GREAT SLAUGHTER'

Wayne bent over them again, evidently puzzled; then he
looked at the dates. They were both dated in August
fifteen years before.

'Why do you keep these old things?' he said, startled
entirely out of his absurd tact of mysticism. 'Why do you
hang them outside your shop?'

'Because,' said the other, simply, 'they are the records of
the last war. You mentioned war just now. It happens to
be my hobby.'

Wayne lifted his large blue eyes with an infantile wonder.

'Come with me,' said Turnbull, shortly, and led him into a parlour at the back of the shop.

In the centre of the parlour stood a large deal table. On it were set rows and rows of the tin and lead soldiers which were part of the shopkeeper's stock. The visitor would have thought nothing of it if it had not been for a certain odd grouping of them, which did not seem either entirely commercial or entirely haphazard.

'You are acquainted, no doubt,' said Turnbull, turning his big eyes upon Wayne—'you are acquainted, no doubt, with the arrangement of the American and Nicaraguan troops in the last battle.' And he waved his hands towards the table.

'I am afraid not,' said Wayne. 'I——'

'Ah, you were at that time occupied too much, perhaps, with the Dervish affair. You will find it in this corner.' And he pointed to a part of the floor where there was another arrangement of children's soldiers grouped here and there.

'You seem,' said Wayne, 'to be interested in military matters.'

'I am interested in nothing else,' answered the toy-shop keeper, simply.

Wayne appeared convulsed with a singular, suppressed excitement.

'In that case,' he said, 'I may approach you with an unusual degree of confidence. Touching the matter of the defence of Notting Hill, I——'

'Defence of Notting Hill? Yes, sir. This way, sir,' said Turnbull, with great perturbation. 'Just step into this side room;' and he led Wayne into another apartment, in which the table was entirely covered with an arrangement of children's bricks. A second glance at it told Wayne that the bricks were arranged in the form of a precise and perfect plan of Notting Hill. 'Sir,' said Turnbull, impressively, 'you have, by a kind of accident, hit upon the whole secret of my life. As a boy, I grew up among the last wars of the world, when Nicaragua was taken and the dervishes wiped out. And I adopted it as a hobby, sir, as you might adopt astronomy or bird-stuffing. I had no ill-will to any one, but I was interested in war as a science, as a game. And suddenly I was bowled out. The big Powers of the world, having swallowed up all the small ones, came to that confounded agreement, and there was no more war. There was nothing more for me to do but to do what I do now—to read the old campaigns in dirty old newspapers, and to work them out with tin soldiers. One other thing had occurred to me. I thought it an amusing fancy to make a plan of how this district of ours ought to be defended if it were ever attacked. It seems to interest you too.'

'If it were ever attacked,' repeated Wayne, awed into an almost mechanical enunciation. 'Mr. Turnbull, it is attacked. Thank Heaven I am bringing to at least one human being the news that is at bottom the only good news to any son of Adam. Your life has not been useless. Your work has not been play. Now, when the hair is already grey on your head, Turnbull, you shall have your youth. God has not destroyed it, He has only deferred it. Let us sit down here, and you shall explain to me this military map of Notting Hill. For you and I have to defend Notting Hill together.'

Mr. Turnbull looked at the other for a moment, then hesitated, and then sat down beside the bricks and the

D*

stranger. He did not rise again for seven hours, when the dawn broke.

.   .   .   .   .   .

The headquarters of Provost Adam Wayne and his Commander-in-Chief consisted of a small and somewhat unsuccessful milk-shop at the corner of Pump Street. The blank white morning had only just begun to break over the blank London buildings when Wayne and Turnbull were to be found seated in the cheerless and unswept shop. Wayne had something feminine in his character; he belonged to that class of persons who forget their meals when anything interesting is in hand. He had had nothing for sixteen hours but hurried glasses of milk, and, with a glass standing empty beside him, he was writing and sketching and dotting and crossing out with inconceivable rapidity with a pencil and a piece of paper. Turnbull was of that more masculine type in which a sense of responsibility increases the appetite, and with his sketch-map beside him he was dealing strenuously with a pile of sandwiches in a paper packet, and a tankard of ale from the tavern opposite, whose shutters had just been taken down. Neither of them spoke, and there was no sound in the living stillness except the scratching of Wayne's pencil and the squealing of an aimless-looking cat. At length Wayne broke the silence by saying—

'Seventeen pounds, eight shillings and ninepence.'

Turnbull nodded and put his head in the tankard.

'That,' said Wayne, 'is not counting the five pounds you took yesterday. What did you do with it?'

'Ah, that is rather interesting!' replied Turnbull, with his mouth full. 'I used that five pounds in a kindly and philanthropic act.'

Wayne was gazing with mystification in his queer and innocent eyes.

'I used that five pounds,' continued the other, 'in giving no less than forty little London boys rides in hansom cabs.'

'Are you insane?' asked the Provost.

'It is only my light touch,' returned Turnbull. 'These hansom-cab rides will raise the tone—raise the tone, my dear fellow—of our London youths, widen their horizon, brace their nervous system, make them acquainted with the various public monuments of our great city. Education, Wayne, education. How many excellent thinkers have pointed out that political reform is useless until we produce a cultured populace. So that twenty years hence, when these boys are grown up——'

'Mad!' said Wayne, laying down his pencil; 'and five pounds gone!'

'You are in error,' explained Turnbull. 'You grave creatures can never be brought to understand how much quicker work really goes with the assistance of nonsense and good meals. Stripped of its decorative beauties, my statement was strictly accurate. Last night I gave forty half-crowns to forty little boys, and sent them all over London to take hansom cabs. I told them in every case to tell the cabman to bring them to this spot. In half an hour from now the declaration of war will be posted up. At the same time the cabs will have begun to come in, you will have ordered out the guard, the little boys will drive up in state, we shall commandeer the horses for cavalry, use the cabs for barricade, and give the men the choice between serving in our ranks and detention in our basements and cellars. The little boys we can use as scouts. The main thing is that we start the war with an advantage unknown in all the

other armies—horses. And now,' he said, finishing his
beer, 'I will go and drill the troops.'

And he walked out of the milk-shop, leaving the Provost
staring.

A minute or two afterwards, the Provost laughed. He
only laughed once or twice in his life, and then he did it in
a queer way as if it were an art he had not mastered. Even
he saw something funny in the preposterous coup of the
half-crowns and the little boys. He did not see the mon-
strous absurdity of the whole policy and the whole war.
He enjoyed it seriously as a crusade, that is, he enjoyed it
far more than any joke can be enjoyed. Turnbull enjoyed
it partly as a joke, even more perhaps as a reversion from
the things he hated—modernity and monotony and civilisation. To break up the vast machinery of modern life and
use the fragments as engines of war, to make the barricade
of omnibuses and points of vantage of chimney-pots, was
to him a game worth infinite risk and trouble. He had that
rational and deliberate preference which will always to the
end trouble the peace of the world, the rational and deliberate preference for a short life and a merry one.

CHAPTER III

The Experiment of Mr. Buck

AN earnest and eloquent petition was sent up to the King signed with the names of Wilson, Barker, Buck, Swindon and others. It urged that at the forthcoming conference to be held in his Majesty's presence touching the final disposition of the property in Pump Street, it might be held not inconsistent with political decorum and with the unutterable respect they entertained for his Majesty if they appeared in ordinary morning dress, without the costume decreed for them as Provosts. So it happened that the company appeared at that council in frock coats and the King himself limited his love of ceremony to appearing (after his not unusual manner) in evening dress with one order—in this case not the Garter, but the button of the Club of Old Clipper's Best Pals, a decoration obtained (with difficulty) from a half-penny boy's paper. Thus also it happened that the only spot of colour in the room was Adam Wayne, who entered in great dignity with the great red robes and the great sword.

'We have met,' said Auberon, 'to decide the most arduous of modern problems. May we be successful.' And he sat down gravely.

Buck turned his chair a little and flung one leg over the other.

'Your Majesty,' he said, quite good-humouredly, 'there is only one thing I can't understand, and that is why this affair is not settled in five minutes. Here's a small property which is worth a thousand to us and is not worth a hundred to any one else. We offer the thousand. It's not business-like, I know, for we ought to get it for less, and it's not reasonable and it's not fair on us, but I'm damned if I can see why it's difficult.'

'The difficulty may be very simply stated,' said Wayne. 'You may offer a million and it will be very difficult for you to get Pump Street.'

'But, look here, Mr. Wayne,' cried Barker, striking in with a kind of cold excitement. 'Just look here. You've no right to take up a position like that. You've a right to stand out for a bigger price, but you aren't doing that. You're refusing what you and every sane man knows to be a splendid offer simply from malice or spite—it must be malice or spite. And that kind of thing is really criminal; it's against the public good. The King's Government would be justified in forcing you.'

With his lean fingers spread on the table he stared anxiously at Wayne's face, which did not move.

'In forcing you . . . it would,' he repeated.

'It shall,' said Buck, shortly, turning to the table with a jerk. 'We have done our best to be decent.'

Wayne lifted his large eyes slowly.

'Was it my Lord Buck,' he enquired, 'who said that the King of England "shall" do something?'

Buck flushed and said testily—

'I mean it must—it ought to, as I say we've done our best to be generous. I defy any one to deny it. As it is Mr. Wayne, I don't want to say a word that's uncivil. I hope it's not uncivil to say that you can be, and ought to be, in gaol. It is criminal to stop public works for a whim. A man might as well burn ten thousand onions in his front garden or bring up his children to run naked in the street, as do what you say you have a right to do. People have been compelled to sell before now. The King could compel you, and I hope he will.'

'Until he does,' said Wayne, calmly, 'the power and government of this great nation is on my side and not yours, and I defy you to defy it.'

'In what sense,' cried Barker, with his feverish eyes and hands, 'is the Government on your side?'

With one ringing movement Wayne unrolled a great parchment on the table. It was decorated down the sides with wild water-colour sketches of vestrymen in crowns and wreaths.

'The Charter of the Cities,' he began.

Buck exploded in a brutal oath and laughed.

'That tomfool's joke. Haven't we had enough——'

'And there you sit,' cried Wayne, springing erect and with a voice like a trumpet, 'with no argument but to insult the King before his face.'

Buck rose also with blazing eyes.

'I am hard to bully,' he began—and the slow tones of the King struck in with incomparable gravity—

'My Lord Buck, I must ask you to remember that your King is present. It is not often that he needs to protect himself among his subjects.'

Barker turned to him with frantic gestures.

'For God's sake don't back up the madman now,' he implored. 'Have your joke another time. Oh, for Heaven's sake——'

'My Lord Provost of South Kensington,' said King Auberon, steadily. 'I do not follow your remarks which are uttered with a rapidity unusual at Court. Nor do your well-meant efforts to convey the rest with your fingers materially assist me. I say that my Lord Provost of North Kensington, to whom I spoke, ought not in the presence of his Sovereign to speak disrespectfully of his Sovereign's ordinances. Do you disagree?'

Barker turned restlessly in his chair, and Buck cursed without speaking. The King went on in a comfortable voice—

'My Lord Provost of Notting Hill, proceed.'

Wayne turned his blue eyes on the King, and to every one's surprise there was a look in them not of triumph, but of a certain childish distress.

'I am sorry, your Majesty,' he said; 'I fear I was more than equally to blame with the Lord Provost of North Kensington. We are debating somewhat eagerly, and we both rose to our feet. I did so first, I am ashamed to say. The Provost of North Kensington is, therefore, comparatively innocent. I beseech your Majesty to address your rebuke chiefly, at least, to me. Mr. Buck is not innocent, for he did no doubt, in the heat of the moment, speak disrespectfully. But the rest of the discussion he seems to me to have conducted with great good temper.'

Buck looked genuinely pleased, for business men are all simple-minded, and have therefore that degree of communion with fanatics. The King, for some reason, looked, for the first time in his life, ashamed.

'This very kind speech of the Provost of Notting Hill,' began Buck, pleasantly, 'seems to me to show that we have at last got on to a friendly footing. Now come, Mr. Wayne. Five hundred pounds have been offered to you for a property you admit not to be worth a hundred. Well, I am a rich man and I won't be outdone in generosity. Let us say fifteen hundred pounds, and have done with it. And let us shake hands.' And he rose, glowing and laughing.

'Fifteen hundred pounds,' whispered Mr. Wilson of Bayswater; 'can we do fifteen hundred pounds?'

'I'll stand the racket,' said Buck heartily. 'Mr. Wayne is a gentleman and has spoken up for me. So I suppose the negotiations are at an end.'

Wayne bowed.

'They are indeed at an end. I am sorry I cannot sell you the property.'

'What?' cried Mr. Barker, starting to his feet.

'Mr. Buck has spoken correctly,' said the King.

'I have, I have,' cried Buck, springing up also; 'I said——'

'Mr. Buck has spoken correctly,' said the King; 'the negotiations are at an end.'

All the men at the table rose to their feet; Wayne alone rose without excitement.

'Have I, then,' he said, 'your Majesty's permission to depart? I have given my last answer.'

'You have it,' said Auberon, smiling, but not lifting his eyes from the table. And amid a dead silence the Provost of Notting Hill passed out of the room.

'Well?' said Wilson, turning round to Barker. 'Well?'

Barker shook his head desperately.

'The man ought to be in an asylum,' he said. 'But one thing is clear, we need not bother further about him. The man can be treated as mad.'

'Of course,' said Buck, turning to him with sombre decisiveness. 'You're perfectly right, Barker. He is a good enough fellow, but he can be treated as mad. Let's put it in simple form. Go and tell any twelve men in any town, go and tell any doctor in any town, that there is a man offered fifteen hundred pounds for a thing he could sell commonly for four hundred, and that when asked for a reason for not accepting it he pleads the inviolate sanctity of Notting Hill and calls it the Holy Mountain. What would they say? What more can we have on our side than the common sense of everybody? On what else do all laws rest? I'll tell you, Barker, what's better than any further discussion. Let's send in workmen on the spot to pull down Pump Street. And if old Wayne says a word, arrest him as a lunatic. That's all.'

Barker's eyes kindled.

'I always regarded you, Buck, if you don't mind my saying so, as a very strong man. I'll follow you.'

'So, of course, will I,' said Wilson.

Buck rose again impulsively.

'Your Majesty,' he said, glowing with popularity, 'I beseech your Majesty to consider favourably the proposal to which we have committed ourselves. Your Majesty's leniency, our own offers, have fallen in vain on that extraordinary man. He may be right. He may be God. He may be the devil. But we think it, for practical purposes, more probable that he is off his head. Unless that assumption were acted on, all human affairs would go to pieces. We act on it, and we propose to start operations in Notting Hill at once.'

The King leaned back in his chair.

'The Charter of the Cities. . . .' he said with a rich intonation.

But Buck, being finally serious, was also cautious, and did not again make the mistake of disrespect.

'Your Majesty,' he said, bowing, 'I am not here to say a word against anything your Majesty has said or done. You are a far better educated man than I, and no doubt there were reasons, upon intellectual grounds, for those proceedings. But may I ask you and appeal to your common good-nature for a sincere answer? When you drew up the Charter of the Cities did you contemplate the rise of a man like Adam Wayne? Did you expect that the Charter—whether it was an experiment, or a scheme of decoration, or a joke—could ever really come to this—to stopping a vast scheme of ordinary business, to shutting up a road, to spoiling the chances of cabs, omnibuses, railway stations, to disorganising half a city, to risking a kind of civil war? Whatever were your objects, were they that?'

Barker and Wilson looked at him admiringly; the King more admiringly still.

'Provost Buck,' said Auberon, 'you speak in public uncommonly well. I give you your point with the magnanimity of an artist. My scheme did not include the appearance of Mr. Wayne. Alas! would that my poetic power had been great enough.'

'I thank your Majesty,' said Buck, courteously but quickly. 'Your Majesty's statements are always clear and studied: therefore I may draw a deduction. As the scheme, whatever it was, on which you set your heart did not include the appearance of Mr. Wayne, it will survive his removal. Why not let us clear away this particular Pump Street, which does interfere with our plans, and which does not, by your Majesty's own statement, interfere with yours.'

'Caught out!' said the King, enthusiastically and quite impersonally, as if he were watching a cricket match.

'This man Wayne,' continued Buck, 'would be shut up by any doctors in England. But we only ask to have it put before them. Meanwhile no one's interests, not even in all probability his own, can be really damaged by going on with the improvements in Notting Hill. Not our interests, of course, for it has been the hard and quiet work of ten years. Not the interests of Notting Hill, for nearly all its educated inhabitants desire the change. Not the interests of your Majesty, for you say, with characteristic sense, that you never contemplated the rise of the lunatic at all. Not, as I say, his own interests, for the man has a kind heart and many talents, and a couple of good doctors would probably put him righter than all the free cities and sacred mountains in creation. I therefore assume, if I may use so bold a word, that your Majesty will not offer any obstacle to our proceeding with the improvements.'

And Mr. Buck sat down amid subdued but excited applause among the allies.

'Mr. Buck,' said the King, 'I beg your pardon, for a number of beautiful and sacred thoughts, in which you were generally classified as a fool. But there is another thing to be considered. Suppose you send in your workmen, and Mr. Wayne does a thing regrettable indeed, but of which, I am sorry to say, I think him quite capable—knocks their teeth out.'

'I have thought of that, your Majesty,' said Mr. Buck, easily, 'and I think it can simply be guarded against. Let us send in a strong guard of say a hundred men—a hundred of the North Kensington Halberdiers' (he smiled grimly), 'of whom your Majesty is so fond. Or say—a hundred and fifty. The whole population of Pump Street, I fancy, is only about a hundred.'

'Still they might stand together and lick you,' said the King, dubiously.

'Then say two hundred,' said Buck, gaily.

'It might happen,' said the King, restlessly, 'that one Notting Hiller fought better than two North Kensingtons.'

'It might,' said Buck, coolly; 'then say two hundred and fifty.'

The King bit his lip.

'And if they are beaten, too,' he said viciously.

'Your Majesty,' said Buck, and leaned back easily in his chair. 'Suppose they are. If anything be clear, it is clear that all fighting matters are mere matters of arithmetic. Here we have a hundred and fifty say of Notting Hill soldiers. Or say two hundred. If one of them can fight two of us—we can send in, not four hundred, but six hundred, and smash him. That is all. It is out of all immediate probability that one of them could fight four of us. So what I say is this. Run no risks. Finish it at once. Send in eight hundred men and smash him—smash him almost without seeing him. And go on with the improvements.'

And Mr. Buck pulled out a bandanna and blew his nose.

'Do you know, Mr. Buck,' said the King, staring gloomily at the table, 'the admirable clearness of your reason produces in my mind a sentiment which I trust I shall not offend you by describing as an aspiration to punch your head. You irritate me sublimely. What can it be in me? Is it the relic of a moral sense?'

'But your Majesty,' said Barker, eagerly and suavely, 'does not refuse our proposals?'

'My dear Barker, your proposals are as damnable as your manners. I want to have nothing to do with them. Suppose I stopped them altogether. What would happen?'

Barker answered in a very low voice—

'Revolution.'

The King glanced quickly at the men around the table. They were all looking down silently: their brows were red.

He rose with a startling suddenness, and an unusual pallor.

'Gentlemen,' he said, 'you have overruled me. Therefore I can speak plainly. I think Adam Wayne, who is as mad as a hatter, worth more than a million of you. But you have the force, and, I admit, the common sense, and he is lost. Take your eight hundred halberdiers and smash him. It would be more sportsmanlike to take two hundred.'

'More sportsmanlike,' said Buck, grimly, 'but a great deal less humane. We are not artists, and streets purple with gore do not catch our eye in the right way.'

'It is pitiful,' said Auberon. 'With five or six times their number there will be no fight at all.'

'I hope not,' said Buck, rising and adjusting his gloves. 'We desire no fight, your Majesty. We are peaceable business men.'

'Well,' said the King, wearily, 'the conference is at an end at last.'

And he went out of the room before any one else could stir.

.   .   .   .   .   .

Forty workmen, a hundred Bayswater Halberdiers, two hundred from South, and three from North Kensington, assembled at the foot of Holland Walk and marched up it, under the general direction of Barker, who looked flushed and happy in full dress. At the end of the procession a small and sulky figure lingered like an urchin. It was the King.

'Barker,' he said at length, appealing, 'you are an old friend of mine—you understand my hobbies as I understand yours. Why can't you let it alone? I hoped that such fun might come out of this Wayne business. Why can't you let it alone? It doesn't really so much matter to you—what's a road or so? For me it's the one joke that may save me from pessimism. Take fewer men and give me an hour's fun. Really and truly, James, if you collected coins or humming-birds, and I could buy one with the price of your road, I would buy it. I collect incidents—those rare, those precious things. Let me have one. Pay a few pounds for it. Give these Notting Hillers a chance. Let them alone.'

'Auberon,' said Barker, kindly, forgetting all royal titles in a rare moment of sincerity, 'I do feel what you mean. I have had moments when these hobbies have hit me. I have had moments when I have sympathised with your humours. I have had moments, though you may not easily believe it, when I have sympathised with the madness of Adam Wayne. But the world, Auberon, the real world, is not run on these hobbies. It goes on great brutal wheels of facts—wheels on which you are the butterfly. And Wayne is the fly on the wheel.'

Auberon's eyes looked frankly at the other's.

'Thank you, James; what you say is true. It is only a parenthetical consolation to me to compare the intelligence of flies somewhat favourably with the intelligence of wheels. But it is the nature of flies to die soon, and the nature of wheels to go on for ever. Go on with the wheel. Good-bye, old man.'

And James Barker went on, laughing, with a high colour, slapping his bamboo on his leg.

The King watched the tail of the retreating regiment with a look of genuine depression, which made him seem more like a baby than ever. Then he swung round and struck his hands together.

'In a world without humour,' he said, 'the only thing to do is to eat. And how perfect an exception! How can these people strike dignified attitudes, and pretend that things matter, when the total ludicrousness of life is proved by the very method by which it is supported? A man strikes the lyre, and says, "Life is real, life is earnest," and then goes into a room and stuffs alien substances into a hole in his head. I think Nature was indeed a little broad in her humour in these matters. But we all fall back on the pantomime, as I have in this municipal affair. Nature has her farces, like the act of eating or the shape of the kangaroo, for the more brutal appetite. She keeps her stars and mountains for those who can appreciate something more subtly ridiculous.' He turned to his equerry. 'But, as I said "eating," let us have a picnic like two nice little children. Just run and bring me a table and a dozen courses or so, and plenty of champagne, and under these swinging boughs, Bowler, we will return to Nature.'

It took about an hour to erect in Holland Lane the monarch's simple repast, during which time he walked up and down and whistled, but still with an unaffected air of gloom. He had really been done out of a pleasure he had promised himself, and had that empty and sickened feeling which a child has when disappointed of a pantomime. When he and the equerry had sat down, however, and consumed a fair amount of dry champagne, his spirits began mildly to revive.

'Things take too long in this world,' he said. 'I detest

all this Barkerian business about evolution and the gradual
modification of things. I wish the world had been made
in six days and knocked to pieces again in six more. And
I wish I had done it. The joke's good enough in a broad
way, sun and moon and the image of God, and all that, but
they keep it up so damnably long. Did you ever long for a
miracle, Bowler?'

'No, sir,' said Bowler, who was an evolutionist, and had
been carefully brought up.

'Then I have,' answered the King. 'I have walked along
a street with the best cigar in the cosmos in my mouth, and
more Burgundy inside me than you ever saw in your life,
and longed that the lamp-post would turn into an elephant
to save me from the hell of blank existence. Take my word
for it, my evolutionary Bowler, don't you believe people
when they tell you that people sought for a sign, and
believed in miracles because they were ignorant. They did
it because they were wise, filthily, vilely wise—too wise to
eat or sleep or put on their boots with patience. This
seems delightfully like a new theory of the origin of
Christianity, which would itself be a thing of no mean
absurdity. Take some more wine.'

The wind blew round them as they sat at their little
table, with its white cloth and bright wine-cups, and flung
the tree-tops of Holland Park against each other, but the
sun was in that strong temper which turns green into gold.
The King pushed away his plate, lit a cigar slowly, and
went on—

'Yesterday I thought that something next door to a
really entertaining miracle might happen to me before I
went to amuse the worms. To see that red-haired maniac
waving a great sword, and making speeches to his incom-

parable followers, would have been a glimpse of that Land of Youth from which the Fates shut us out. I had planned some quite delightful things. A Congress of Knightsbridge with a treaty, and myself in the chair, and perhaps a Roman triumph, with jolly old Barker led in chains. And now these wretched prigs have gone and stamped out the exquisite Mr. Wayne altogether, and I suppose they will put him in a private asylum somewhere in their damned humane way. Think of the treasures daily poured out to his unappreciative keeper! I wonder whether they would let me be his keeper. But life is a vale. Never forget at any moment of your existence to regard it in the light of a vale. This graceful habit, if not acquired in youth——'

The King stopped, with his cigar lifted, for there had slid into his eyes the startled look of a man listening. He did not move for a few moments; then he turned his head sharply towards the high, thin, and lath-like paling which fenced certain long gardens and similar spaces from the lane. From behind it there was coming a curious scrambling and scraping noise, as of a desperate thing imprisoned in this box of thin wood. The King threw away his cigar, and jumped on to the table. From this position he saw a pair of hands hanging with a hungry clutch on the top of the fence. Then the hands quivered with a convulsive effort, and a head shot up between them—the head of one of the Bayswater Town Council, his eyes and whiskers wild with fear. He swung himself over, and fell on the other side on his face, and groaned openly and without ceasing. The next moment the thin, taut wood of the fence was struck as by a bullet, so that it reverberated like a drum, and over it came tearing and cursing, with torn clothes and broken nails and bleeding faces, twenty men at one rush. The King sprang five feet clear off the table on to the ground. The moment after the table was flung over, sending bottles and glasses flying, and the *débris* was literally swept along the ground by that stream of men pouring past, and Bowler was borne along with them, as the King said in his famous newspaper article, 'like a captured bride.' The great fence swung and split under the load of climbers that still scaled and cleared it. Tremendous gaps were torn in it by this living artillery; and through them the King could see more and more frantic faces, as in a dream, and more and more men running. They were as miscellaneous as if some one had taken the lid off a human dustbin. Some were untouched, some were slashed and battered and bloody, some were splendidly dressed, some tattered and half-naked, some were in the fantastic garb of the burlesque cities, some in the dullest modern dress. The King stared at all of them, but none of them looked at the King. Suddenly he stepped forward.

'Barker,' he said, 'what is all this?'

'Beaten,' said the politician—'beaten all to hell!' And he plunged past with nostrils shaking like a horse's, and more men plunged after him.

Almost as he spoke the last standing strip of fence bowed and snapped, flinging, as from a catapult, a new figure upon the road. He wore the flaming red of the halberdiers of Notting Hill, and on his weapon there was blood, and in his face victory. In another moment masses of red glowed through the gaps of the fence, and the pursuers, with their halberds, came pouring down the lane. Pursued and pursuers alike swept by the little figure with the owlish eyes, who had not taken his hands out of his pockets.

The King had still little beyond the confused sense of a
man caught in a torrent—the feeling of men eddying by.
Then something happened which he was never able afterwards to describe, and which we cannot describe for him.
Suddenly in the dark entrance, between the broken gates of
a garden, there appeared framed a flaming figure.

Adam Wayne, the conqueror, with his face flung back,
and his mane like a lion's, stood with his great sword
point upwards, the red raiment of his office flapping round
him like the red wings of an archangel. And the King
saw, he knew not how, something new and overwhelming.
The great green trees and and the great red robes swung together in the wind. The sword seemed made for the sunlight. The preposterous masquerade, born of his own
mockery, towered over him and embraced the world.
This was the normal, this was sanity, this was nature; and
he himself, with his rationality and his detachment and his
black frock coat, he was the exception and the accident—
a blot of black upon a world of crimson and gold.

BOOK FOUR

*

CHAPTER I

The Battle of the Lamps

MR. BUCK, who, though retired, frequently went down to his big drapery stores in Kensington High Street, was locking up those premises, being the last to leave. It was a wonderful evening of green and gold, but that did not trouble him very much. If you had pointed it out, he would have agreed seriously, for the rich always desire to be artistic.

He stepped out into the cool air, buttoning up his light coat, and blowing great clouds from his cigar, when a figure dashed up to him in another yellow overcoat, but unbuttoned and flying behind him.

'Hullo, Barker!' said the draper. 'Any of our summer articles? You're too late. Factory Acts, Barker. Humanity and progress, my boy.'

'Oh, don't chatter,' cried Barker, stamping. 'We've been beaten.'

'Beaten—by what?' asked Buck, mystified.

'By Wayne.'

Buck looked at Barker's fierce white face for the first time, as it gleamed in the lamplight.

'Come and have a drink,' he said.

They adjourned to a cushioned and glaring buffet, and Buck established himself slowly and lazily in a seat, and pulled out his cigar-case.

'Have a smoke,' he said.

Barker was still standing, and on the fret, but after a moment's hesitation, he sat down, as if he might spring up again the next minute. They ordered drinks in silence.

'How did it happen?' asked Buck, turning his big bold eyes on him.

'How the devil do I know?' cried Barker. 'It happened like—like a dream. How can two hundred men beat six hundred? How can they?'

'Well,' said Buck, coolly. 'How did they? You ought to know.'

'I don't know. I can't describe,' said the other, drumming on the table. 'It seemed like this. We were six hundred and marched with those damned poleaxes of Auberon's—the only weapons we've got. We marched two abreast. We went up to Holland Walk, between the high palings which seemed to me to go straight as an arrow for Pump Street. I was near the tail of the line and it was a long one. When the end of it was still between the high palings, the head of the line was already crossing Holland Park Avenue. Then the head plunged into the network of narrow streets on the other side, and the tail and myself came out on the great crossing. When we also had reached the northern side and turned up a small street that points, crookedly as it were, towards Pump Street, the whole thing felt different. The streets dodged and bent so much that the head of our line seemed lost altogether: it might as well have been in North America. And all this time we hadn't seen a soul.'

Buck, who was idly dabbing the ash of his cigar on the ash-tray, began to move it deliberately over the table, making feathery grey lines, a kind of map.

'But though the little streets were all deserted (which

got a trifle on my nerves), as we got deeper and deeper into
them, a thing began to happen that I couldn't understand.
Sometimes a long way ahead—three turns of corners ahead,
as it were—there broke suddenly a sort of noise, clattering,
and confused cries, and then stopped. Then, when it
happened, something, I can't describe it—a kind of shake
or stagger went down the line, as if the line were a live
thing, whose head had been struck, or had been an electric
cord. None of us knew why we were moving, but we
moved and jostled. Then we recovered, and went on
through the little dirty streets, round corners, and up
twisted ways. The little crooked streets began to give me
a feeling I can't explain—as if it were a dream. I felt as if
things had lost their reason, and we should never get out of
the maze. Odd to hear me talk like that, isn't it? The
streets were quite well-known streets, all down on the map.
But the fact remains. I wasn't afraid of something happening. I was afraid of nothing ever happening—nothing ever
happening for all God's eternity.'

He drained his glass and called for more whisky. He
drank it and went on.

'And then something did happen. Buck, it's the solemn
truth, that nothing has ever happened to you in your life.
Nothing has ever happened to me in my life.'

'Nothing ever happened!' said Buck, staring. 'What do
you mean?'

'Nothing has ever happened,' repeated Barker, with a
morbid obstinacy. 'You don't know what a thing happening means? You sit in your office expecting customers,
and customers come; you walk in the street expecting
friends, and friends meet you; you want a drink and get it;
you feel inclined for a bet and make it. You expect either

to win or lose, and you do either one or the other. But things happening!' and he shuddered ungovernably.

'Go on,' said Buck, shortly. 'Get on.'

'As we walked wearily round the corners, something happened. When something happens, it happens first, and you see it afterwards. It happens of itself, and you have nothing to do with it. It proves a dreadful thing—that there are other things besides one's self. I can only put it in this way. We went round one turning, two turnings, three turnings, four turnings, five. Then I lifted myself slowly up from the gutter where I had been shot half senseless, and was beaten down again by living men crashing on top of me, and the world was full of roaring, and big men rolling about like ninepins.'

Buck looked at his map with knitted brows.

'Was that Portobello Road?' he asked.

'Yes,' said Barker. 'Yes; Portobello Road—I saw it afterwards; but, my God—what a place it was! Buck, have you ever stood and let a six foot of a man lash and lash at your head with six feet of pole with six pounds of steel at the end? Because, when you have had that experience, as Walt Whitman says, "you re-examine philosophies and religions." '

'I have no doubt,' said Buck. 'If that was Portobello Road, don't you see what happened?'

'I know what happened exceedingly well. I was knocked down four times; an experience which, as I say, has an effect on the mental attitude. And another thing happened, too. I knocked down two men. After the fourth fall (there was not much bloodshed—more brutal rushing and throwing—for nobody could use their weapons), after the fourth fall, I say, I got up like a devil, and I tore a poleaxe out of a man's hand and struck where I saw the scarlet of Wayne's fellows, struck again and again. Two of them went over, bleeding on the stones, thank God—and I laughed and found myself sprawling in the gutter again, and got up again, and struck again, and broke my halberd to pieces. I hurt a man's head, though.'

Buck set down his glass with a bang, and spat out curses through his thick moustache.

'What is the matter?' asked Barker, stopping, for the man had been calm up to now, and now, his agitation was far more violent than his own.

'The matter?' said Buck, bitterly; 'don't you see how these maniacs have got us? Why should two idiots, one a clown and the other a screaming lunatic, make sane men so different from themselves? Look here, Barker; I will give you a picture. A very well-bred young man of this century is dancing about in a frock-coat. He has in his hands a nonsensical seventeenth-century halberd, with which he is trying to kill men in a street in Notting Hill. Damn it! don't you see how they've got us? Never mind how you felt—that is how you looked. The King would put his cursed head on one side and call it exquisite. The Provost of Notting Hill would put his cursed nose in the air and call it heroic. But in Heaven's name what would you have called it—two days before?'

Barker bit his lip.

'You haven't been through it, Buck,' he said. 'You don't understand fighting—the atmosphere.'

'I don't deny the atmosphere,' said Buck, striking the table. 'I only say it's their atmosphere. It's Adam Wayne's atmosphere. It's the atmosphere which you and I thought had vanished from an educated world for ever.'

E

'Well, it hasn't,' said Barker; 'and if you have any lingering doubts, lend me a poleaxe and I'll show you.'

There was a long silence, and then Buck turned to his neighbour and spoke in that good-tempered tone that comes of a power of looking facts in the face; the tone in which he concluded great bargains.

'Barker,' he said, 'you are right. This old thing—this fighting, has come back. It has come back suddenly and taken us by surprise. So it is first blood to Adam Wayne. But, unless reason and arithmetic and everything else have gone crazy, it must be next and last blood to us. But when an issue has really arisen, there is only one thing to do—to study that issue as such and win in it. Barker, since it is fighting, we must understand fighting. I must understand fighting as coolly and completely as I understand drapery; you must understand fighting as coolly and completely as you understand politics. Now, look at the facts. I stick without hesitation to my original formula. Fighting, when we have the stronger force, is only a matter of arithmetic. It must be. You asked me just now how two hundred men could defeat six hundred. I can tell you. Two hundred men can defeat six hundred when the six hundred behave like fools. When they forget the very conditions they are fighting in; when they fight in a swamp as if it were a mountain; when they fight in a forest as if it were a plain; when they fight in streets without remembering the object of streets.'

'What is the object of streets?' asked Barker.

'What is the object of supper?' cried Buck, furiously. 'Isn't it obvious? This military science is mere common sense. The object of a street is to lead from one place to

another; therefore all streets join; therefore street fighting
is quite a peculiar thing. You advanced into that hive of
streets as if you were advancing into an open plain where
you could see everything. Instead of that you were advancing into the bowels of a fortress, with streets pointing at
you, streets turning on you, streets jumping out at you, and
all in the hands of the enemy. Do you know what Portobello Road is? It is the only point on your journey where
two side streets run up opposite each other. Wayne
massed his men on the two sides, and when he had let
enough of your line go past, cut it in two like a worm.
Don't you see what would have saved you?'

Barker shook his head.

'Can't your "atmosphere" help you?' asked Buck,
bitterly. 'Must I attempt explanations in the romantic
manner? Suppose that, as you were fighting blindly with
the red Notting Hillers who imprisoned you on both
sides, you had heard a shout from behind them. Suppose,
oh, romantic Barker! that behind the red tunics you had
seen the blue and gold of South Kensington taking them in
the rear, surrounding them in their turn and hurling them
on to your halberds.'

'If the thing had been possible,' began Barker, cursing.

'The thing would have been as possible,' said Buck,
simply; 'as simple as arithmetic. There are a certain number of street entries that lead to Pump Street. There are
not nine hundred; there are not nine million. They do not
grow in the night. They do not increase like mushrooms.
It must be possible with such an overwhelming force as we
have to advance by all of them at once. In every one of the
arteries, or approaches, we can put almost as many men as
Wayne can put into the field altogether. Once do that and

we have him to demonstration. It is like a proposition in Euclid.'

'You think that is certain,' said Barker, anxious but dominated delightfully.

'I'll tell you what I think,' said Buck, getting up jovially. 'I think Adam Wayne made an uncommonly spirited little fight. And I think I am confoundedly sorry for him.'

'Buck, you are a great man,' cried Barker, rising also. 'You've knocked me sensible again. I am ashamed to say it, but I was getting romantic. Of course, what you say is adamantine sense. Fighting, being physical, must be mathematical. We were beaten because we were neither mathematical nor physical nor anything else—because we deserved to be beaten. Hold all the approaches, and with our force we must have him. When shall we open the next campaign?'

'Now,' said Buck, and walked out of the bar.

'Now!' cried Barker, following him eagerly. 'Do you mean now? It is so late.'

Buck turned on him stamping.

'Do you think fighting is under the Factory Acts?' he said. And he called a cab. 'Notting Hill Gate Station,' he said, and the two drove off.

.   .   .   .   .   .

A genuine reputation can sometimes be made in an hour. Buck, in the next sixty or eighty minutes, showed himself a really great man of action. His cab carried him like a thunderbolt from the King to Wilson, from Wilson to Swindon, from Swindon to Barker again; if his course was jagged, it had the jaggedness of the lightning. Only two things he carried with him, his inevitable cigar and the map of North Kensington and Notting Hill. There were, as he again and again pointed out, with every variety of persuasion and violence, only nine possible ways of approaching Pump Street within a quarter of a mile around it; three out of Westbourne Grove, two out of Ladbroke Grove, and four out of Notting Hill High Street. And he had detachments of two hundred each, stationed at every one of the entrances before the last green of that strange sunset had sunk out of the black sky.

The sky was particularly black, and on this alone was one false protest raised against the triumphant optimism of the Provost of North Kensington. He overruled it with his infectious common sense.

'There is no such thing,' he said, 'as night in London. You have only to follow the line of street lamps. Look, here is the map. Two hundred purple North Kensington soldiers under myself march up Ossington Street, two hundred more under Captain Bruce, of the North Kensington Guard, up Clanricarde Gardens.* Two hundred yellow West Kensingtons under Provost Swindon attack from Pembridge Road. Two hundred more of my men from the eastern streets, leading away from Queen's Road. Two detachments of yellows enter by two roads from Westbourne Grove. Lastly, two hundred green Bayswaters come down from the North through Chepstow Place, and two hundred more under Provost Wilson himself, through the upper part of Pembridge Road. Gentlemen, it is mate in two moves. The enemy must either mass in Pump Street and be cut to pieces—or they must retreat past

---

* Clanricarde Gardens at this time was no longer a *cul-de-sac*, but was connected by Pump Street to Pembridge Square. See map.

the Gaslight & Coke Co.—and rush on my four hundred—
or they must retreat past St. Luke's Church and rush on the
six hundred from the West. Unless we are all mad, it's
plain. Come on. To your quarters and await Captain
Bruce's signal to advance. Then you have only to walk
up a line of gas-lamps and smash this nonsense by
pure mathematics. Tomorrow we shall be all civilians
again.'

His optimism glowed like a great fire in the night, and
ran round the terrible ring in which Wayne was now held
helpless. The fight was already over. One man's energy
for one hour had saved the city from war.

For the next ten minutes Buck walked up and down
silently beside the motionless clump of his two hundred.
He had not changed his appearance in any way, except to
sling across his yellow overcoat a case with a revolver in it.
So that his light-clad modern figure showed up oddly
beside the pompous purple uniforms of his halberdiers,
which darkly but richly coloured the black night.

At length a shrill trumpet rang from some way up the
street; it was the signal of advance. Buck briefly gave the
word, and the whole purple line, with its dimly shining
steel, moved up the side alley. Before it was a slope of
street, long, straight, and shining in the dark. It was a
sword pointed at Pump Street, the heart at which nine
other swords were pointed that night.

A quarter of an hour's silent marching brought them
almost within earshot of any tumult in the doomed citadel.
But still there was no sound and no sign of the enemy. This
time, at any rate, they knew that they were closing in on it
mechanically, and they marched on under the lamplight
and the dark without any of that eerie sense of ignorance

which Barker had felt when entering the hostile country by one avenue alone.

'Halt—point arms!' cried Buck, suddenly, and as he spoke there came a clatter of feet tumbling along the stones. But the halberds were levelled in vain. The figure that rushed up was a messenger from the contingent of the North.

'Victory, Mr. Buck!' he cried, panting, 'they are ousted. Provost Wilson of Bayswater has taken Pump Street.'

Buck ran forward in his excitement.

'Then, which way are they retreating? It must be either by St. Luke's to meet Swindon, or by the Gas Company to meet us. Run like mad to Swindon and see that the yellows are holding the St. Luke's Road. We will hold this, never fear. We have them in an iron trap. Run!'

As the messenger dashed away into the darkness, the great guard of North Kensington swung on with the certainty of a machine. Yet scarcely a hundred yards further their halberd points again fell in line gleaming in the gas-light. For again a clatter of feet was heard on the stones, and again it proved to be only the messenger.

'Mr. Provost,' he said, 'the yellow West Kensingtons have been holding the road by St. Luke's for twenty minutes since the capture of Pump Street. Pump Street is not two hundred yards away, they cannot be retreating down that road.'

'Then they are retreating down this!' said Provost Buck, with a final cheerfulness, 'and by good fortune down a well-lighted road, though it twists about. Forward!'

As they moved along the last three hundred yards of their journey, Buck fell, for the first time in his life, perhaps, into a kind of philosophical reverie, for men of his type are always made kindly, and as it were melancholy, by success.

'I am sorry for poor old Wayne, I really am,' he thought. 'He spoke up splendidly for me at that Council. And he blacked old Barker's eye with considerable spirit. But I don't see what a man can expect when he fights against arithmetic, to say nothing of civilisation. And what a wonderful hoax all this military genius is. I suspect I've just discovered what Cromwell discovered, that a sensible tradesman is the best general, and that a man who can buy men and sell men can lead and kill them. The thing's simply like adding up a column in a ledger. If Wayne has two hundred men, he can't put two hundred men in nine places at once. If they're ousted from Pump Street they're flying somewhere. If they're not flying past the church they're flying past the Works. And so we have them. We business men should have no chance at all except that cleverer people than we get bees in their bonnets that prevent them from reasoning properly—so we reason alone. And so I, who am comparatively stupid, see things as God sees them, as a vast machine. My God, what's this?' And he clapped his hands to his eyes and staggered back.

Then through the darkness he cried in a dreadful voice—

'Did I blaspheme God?—I am struck blind.'

'What?' wailed another voice behind him, the voice of a certain Wilfred Jarvis of North Kensington.

'Blind!' cried Buck; 'blind!'

'I'm blind, too!' cried Jarvis, in an agony.

'Fools, all of you,' said a gross voice behind them; 'we're all blind. The lamps have gone out.'

'The lamps—but why? where?' cried Buck, turning furiously in the darkness. 'How are we to get on? How are we to chase the enemy? Where have they gone?'

'The enemy went——' said the rough voice behind, and then stopped, doubtfully.

'Where?' shouted Buck, stamping like a madman.

'They went,' said the gruff voice, 'past the Gas Works, and they've used their chance.'

'Great God!' thundered Buck, and snatched at his revolver; 'do you mean they've turned out——'

But almost before he had spoken the words, he was hurled like a stone from a catapult into the midst of his own men.

'Notting Hill! Notting Hill!' cried frightful voices out of the darkness, and they seemed to come from all sides, for the men of North Kensington, unacquainted with the road, had lost all their bearings in the black world of blindness.

'Notting Hill! Notting Hill!' cried the invisible people, and the invaders were hewn down horribly with black steel, with steel that gave no glint against any light.

.   .   .   .   .   .

Buck, though badly maimed with the blow of a halberd, kept an angry but splendid sanity. He groped madly for the wall and found it. Struggling with crawling fingers along it, he found a side opening and retreated into it with the remnants of his men. Their adventures during that prodigious night are not to be described. They did not know whether they were going towards or away from the enemy. Not knowing where they themselves were, or where their opponents were, it was mere irony to ask where was the rest of their army. For a thing had descended upon them

E*

which London does not know—darkness, which was
before the stars were made, and they were as much lost in
it as if they had been made before the stars. Every now and
then, as those frightful hours wore on, they buffeted in the
darkness against living men, who struck at them and at
whom they struck, with an idiot fury. When at last the
grey dawn came, they found they had wandered back to
the edge of the Uxbridge Road. They found that in those
horrible eyeless encounters, the North Kensingtons and the
Bayswaters and the West Kensingtons had again and again
met and butchered each other, and they heard that Adam
Wayne was barricaded in Pump Street.

CHAPTER II

The Correspondent of 'The Court Journal'

JOURNALISM had become like most other such things in England, under the cautious government and philosophy represented by James Barker, somewhat sleepy and much diminished in importance. This was partly due to the disappearance of party government and public speaking, partly to the compromise or dead-lock which had made foreign wars impossible, but mostly, of course, to the temper of the whole nation, which was that of a people in a kind of back-water. Perhaps the most well-known of the remaining newspapers was the *Court Journal*, which was published in a dusty but genteel-looking office just out of Kensington High Street. For when all the papers of a people have been for years growing more and more dim and decorous and optimistic, the dimmest and most decorous and most optimistic is very likely to win. In the journalistic competition which was still going on at the beginning of the twentieth century, the final victor was the *Court Journal*.

For some mysterious reason the King had a great affection for hanging about in the *Court Journal* office, smoking a morning cigarette and looking over files. Like all ingrainedly idle men, he was very fond of lounging and chatting in places where other people were doing work. But one would have thought that, even in the prosaic England of his day, he might have found a more bustling centre.

On this particular morning, however, he came out of Kensington Palace with a more alert step and a busier air than usual. He wore an extravagantly long frock-coat, a pale-green waistcoat, a very full and *dégagé* black tie, and curious yellow gloves. This was his uniform as Colonel of a regiment of his own creation, the 1st Decadents Green. It was a beautiful sight to see him drilling them. He walked quickly across the Park and the High Street, lighting his cigarette as he went, and flung open the door of the *Court Journal* office.

'You've heard the news, Pally—you've heard the news?' he said.

The Editor's name was Hoskins, but the King called him Pally, which was an abbreviation of Paladium of our Liberties.

'Well, your Majesty,' said Hoskins, slowly (he was a worried, gentlemanly looking person, with a wandering brown beard)—'well, your Majesty, I have heard rather curious things, but I——'

'You'll hear more of them,' said the King, dancing a few steps of a kind of negro shuffle. 'You'll hear more of them, my blood-and-thunder tribune. Do you know what I am going to do for you?'

'No, your Majesty,' replied the Paladium, vaguely.

'I'm going to put your paper on strong dashing, enter-prising lines, said the King. 'Now, where are your posters of last night's defeat?'

'I did not propose, your Majesty,' said the Editor, 'to have any posters exactly——'

'Paper, paper!' cried the King, wildly; 'bring me paper as big as a house. I'll do you posters. Stop, I must take my coat off.' He began removing that garment with an air of set intensity, flung it playfully at Mr. Hoskins' head, entirely enveloping him, and looked at himself in the glass. 'The coat off,' he said, 'and hat on. That looks like a sub-editor. It is indeed the very essence of sub-editing. Well,' he continued, turning round abruptly, 'come along with that paper.'

The Paladium had only just extricated himself reverently from the folds of the King's frock-coat, and said bewildered—

'I am afraid, your Majesty——'

'Oh, you've got no enterprise,' said Auberon. 'What's that roll in the corner? Wall-paper? Decorations for your private residence? Art in the home, Pally? Fling it over here, and I'll paint such posters on the back of it that when you put it up in your drawing-room you'll paste the original pattern against the wall.' And the King unrolled the wall-paper, spreading it over the whole floor. 'Now give me the scissors,' he cried, and took them himself before the other could stir.

He slit the paper into about five pieces, each nearly as big as a door. Then he took a big blue pencil and went down on his knees on the dusty oil-cloth, and began to write on them, in huge letters—

'FROM THE FRONT

GENERAL BUCK DEFEATED

DARKNESS, DANGER, AND DEATH

WAYNE SAID TO BE IN PUMP STREET

FEELING IN THE CITY'

He contemplated it for some time, with his head on one side, and got up, with a sigh.

'Not quite intense enough,' he said—'not alarming. I

want the *Court Journal* to be feared as well as loved. Let's try something more hard-hitting.' And he went down on his knees again. After sucking the blue pencil for some time, he began writing again busily. 'How will this do?' he said—

'WAYNE'S WONDERFUL VICTORY'

'I suppose,' he said, looking up appealingly, and sucking the pencil—'I suppose we couldn't say "wictory"— "Wayne's wonderful wictory"? No, no. Refinement, Pally, refinement. I have it.'

'WAYNE WINS
ASTOUNDING FIGHT IN THE DARK
The gas-lamps in their courses, fought against Buck.'

'(Nothing like our fine old English translation.) What else can we say? Well, anything to annoy old Buck;' and he added, thoughtfully, in smaller letters—

'Rumoured Court-martial on General Buck.'

'Those will do for the present,' he said, and turned them both face downwards. 'Paste, please.'

The Paladium, with an air of great terror, brought the paste out of an inner room.

The King slabbed it on with the enjoyment of a child messing with treacle. Then taking one of his huge compositions fluttering in each hand, he ran outside, and began pasting them up in prominent positions over the front of the office.

'And now,' said Auberon, entering again with undiminished vivacity—'now for the leading article.'

He picked up another of the large strips of wall-paper,

and, laying it across a desk, pulled out a fountain-pen and began writing with feverish intensity, reading clauses and fragments aloud to himself, and rolling them on his tongue like wine, to see if they had the pure journalistic flavour.

'The news of the disaster to our forces in Notting Hill, awful as it is—(no, distressing as it is), may do some good if it draws attention to the what's-his-name inefficiency (scandalous inefficiency, of course) of the Government's preparations. In our present state of information, it would be premature (what a jolly word!)—it would be premature to cast any reflections upon the conduct of General Buck, whose services upon so many stricken fields (ha, ha!), and whose honourable scars and laurels, give him a right to have judgment upon him at least suspended. But there is one matter on which we must speak plainly. We have been silent on it too long, from feelings, perhaps of mistaken caution, perhaps of mistaken loyalty. This situation would never have arisen but for what we can only call the indefensible conduct of the King. It pains us to say such things, but, speaking as we do in the public interests (I plagiarise from Barker's famous epigram), we shall not shrink because of the distress we may cause to any individual, even the most exalted. At this crucial moment of our country, the voice of the People demands with a single tongue, "Where is the King?" What is he doing while his subjects tear each other in pieces in the streets of a great city? Are his amusements and his dissipations (of which we cannot pretend to be ignorant) so engrossing that he can spare no thought for a perishing nation? It is with a deep sense of our responsibility that we warn that exalted person that neither his great position nor his incomparable talents will save him in the hour of delirium from the fate of all those who, in the madness of luxury or tyranny, have met the English people in the rare day of its wrath.'

'I am now,' said the King, 'going to write an account of the battle by an eye-witness.' And he picked up a fourth sheet of wall-paper. Almost at the same moment Buck strode quickly into the office. He had a bandage round his head.

'I was told,' he said with his usual gruff civility, 'that your Majesty was here.'

'And of all things on earth,' cried the King, with delight, 'here is an eye-witness! An eye-witness who, I regret to observe, has at present only one eye to witness with. Can you write us the special article, Buck? Have you a rich style?'

Buck, with a self-restraint which almost approached politeness, took no notice whatever of the King's maddening geniality.

'I took the liberty, your Majesty,' he said shortly, 'of asking Mr. Barker to come here also.'

As he spoke, indeed, Barker came swinging into the office, with his usual air of hurry.

'What is happening now?' asked Buck, turning to him with a kind of relief.

'Fighting still going on,' said Barker. 'The four hundred from West Kensington were hardly touched last night. They hardly got near the place. Poor Wilson's Bayswater men got cut about, though. They fought confoundedly well. They took Pump Street once. What mad things do happen in the world. To think that of all of us it should be little Wilson with the red whiskers who came out best.'

The King made a note on his paper—

'Romantic Conduct of Mr. Wilson'

'Yes,' said Buck, 'it makes one a bit less proud of one's "h's." '

The King suddenly folded or crumpled up the paper, and put it in his pocket.

'I have an idea,' he said. 'I will be an eye-witness. I will write you such letters from the Front as will be more gorgeous than the real thing. Give me my coat, Paladium. I entered this room a mere King of England. I leave it Special War Correspondent of the *Court Journal*. It is useless to stop me, Pally; it is vain to cling to my knees, Buck; it is hopeless, Barker, to weep upon my neck. "When duty calls"—the remainder of the sentiment escapes me. You will receive my first article this evening by the eight o'clock post.'

And, running out of the office, he jumped upon a blue Bayswater omnibus that went swinging by.

'Well,' said Barker, gloomily, 'well.'

'Barker,' said Buck, 'business may be lower than politics, but war is, as I discovered last night, a long sight more like business. You politicians are such ingrained demagogues that even when you have a despotism you think of nothing but public opinion. So you learn to tack and run, and are afraid of the first breeze. Now we stick to a thing and get it. And our mistakes help us. Look here! at this moment we've beaten Wayne.'

'Beaten Wayne,' repeated Barker.

'Why the dickens not?' cried the other, flinging out his hands. 'Look here. I said last night that we had them by holding the nine entrances. Well, I was wrong. We should have had them but for a singular event—the lamps went out. But for that it was certain. Has it occurred to you, my brilliant Barker, that another singular event has happened since that singular event of the lamps going out?'

'What event?' asked Barker.

'By an astounding coincidence, the sun has risen,' cried out Buck, with a savage air of patience. 'Why the hell aren't we holding all those approaches now, and passing in on them again? It should have been done at sunrise. The confounded doctor wouldn't let me go out. You were in command.'

Barker smiled grimly.

'It is a gratification to me, my dear Buck, to be able to say that we anticipated your suggestions precisely. We went as early as possible to reconnoitre the nine entrances. Unfortunately, while we were fighting each other in the dark, like a lot of drunken navvies, Mr. Wayne's friends were working very hard indeed. Three hundred yards from Pump Street, at every one of those entrances, there is a barricade nearly as high as the houses. They were finishing the last, in Pembridge Road, when we arrived. Our mistakes,' he cried bitterly, and flung his cigarette on the ground. 'It is not we who learn from them.'

There was a silence for a few moments, and Barker lay back wearily in a chair. The office clock ticked exactly in the stillness.

At length Barker said suddenly—

'Buck, does it ever cross your mind what this is all about? The Hammersmith to Maida Vale thoroughfare was an uncommonly good speculation. You and I hoped a great deal from it. But is it worth it? It will cost us thousands to crush this ridiculous riot. Suppose we let it alone?'

'And be thrashed in public by a red-haired madman

whom any two doctors would lock up?' cried out Buck, starting to his feet. 'What do you propose to do, Mr. Barker? To apologise to the admirable Mr. Wayne? To kneel to the Charter of the Cities? To clasp to your bosom the flag of the Red Lion? To kiss in succession every sacred lamp-post that saved Notting Hill? No, by God! My men fought jolly well—they were beaten by a trick. And they'll fight again.'

'Buck,' said Barker, 'I always admired you. And you were quite right in what you said the other day.'

'In what?'

'In saying,' said Barker, rising quietly, 'that we had all got into Adam Wayne's atmosphere and out of our own. My friend, the whole territorial kingdom of Adam Wayne extends to about nine streets, with barricades at the end of them. But the spiritual kingdom of Adam Wayne extends, God knows where—it extends to this office at any rate. The red-haired madman whom any two doctors would lock up is filling this room with his roaring, unreasonable soul. And it was the red-haired madman who said the last word you spoke.'

Buck walked to the window without replying.

'You understand, of course,' he said at last, 'I do not dream of giving in.'

.   .   .   .   .   .

The King, meanwhile, was rattling along on the top of his blue omnibus. The traffic of London as a whole had not, of course, been greatly disturbed by these events, for the affair was treated as a Notting Hill riot, and that area was marked off as if it had been in the hands of a gang of recognised rioters. The blue omnibuses simply went round as they would have done if a road were being mended, and the omnibus on which the correspondent of the *Court Journal* was sitting swept round the corner of Queen's Road, Bayswater.

The King was alone on the top of the vehicle, and was enjoying the speed at which it was going.

'Forward, my beauty, my Arab,' he said, patting the omnibus encouragingly, 'fleetest of all thy bounding tribe. Are thy relations with thy driver, I wonder, those of the Bedouin and his steed? Does he sleep side by side with thee——'

His meditations were broken by a sudden and jarring stoppage. Looking over the edge, he saw that the heads of the horses were being held by men in the uniform of Wayne's army, and heard the voice of an officer calling out orders.

King Auberon descended from the omnibus with dignity. The guard or picket of red halberdiers who had stopped the vehicle did not number more than twenty, and they were under the command of a short, dark, clever-looking young man, conspicuous among the rest as being clad in an ordinary frock-coat, but girt round the waist with a red sash and a long seventeenth-century sword. A shiny silk hat and spectacles completed the outfit in a pleasing manner.

'To whom have I the honour of speaking?' said the King, endeavouring to look like Charles I, in spite of personal difficulties.

The dark man in spectacles lifted his hat with equal gravity.

'My name is Bowles,' he said. 'I am a chemist. I am also a captain of O Company of the army of Notting Hill.

I am distressed at having to incommode you by stopping the omnibus, but this area is covered by our proclamation, and we intercept all traffic. May I ask to whom I have the honour—Why, good gracious, I beg your Majesty's pardon. I am quite overwhelmed at finding myself concerned with the King.'

Auberon put up his hands with indescribable grandeur.

'Not with the King,' he said; 'with the special war correspondent of the *Court Journal*.'

'I beg your Majesty's pardon,' began Mr. Bowles, doubtfully.

'Do you call me Majesty? I repeat,' said Auberon firmly, 'I am a representative of the press. I have chosen, with a deep sense of responsibility, the name of Pinker. I should desire a veil to be drawn over the past.'

'Very well, sir,' said Mr. Bowles, with an air of submission, 'in our eyes the sanctity of the press is at least as great as that of the throne. We desire nothing better than that our wrongs and our glories should be widely known. May I ask, Mr. Pinker, if you have any objection to being presented to the Provost and to General Turnbull?'

'The Provost I have had the honour of meeting,' said Auberon, easily. 'We old journalists, you know, meet everybody. I should be most delighted to have the same honour again. General Turnbull, also, it would be a gratification to know. The younger men are so interesting. We of the old Fleet Street gang lose touch with them.'

'Will you be so good as to step this way?' said the leader of O Company.

'I am always good,' said Mr. Pinker. 'Lead on.'

CHAPTER III

The Great Army of South
Kensington

THE article from the special correspondent of the *Court Journal* arrived in due course, written on very coarse copy-paper in the King's arabesque of hand-writing, in which three words filled a page, and yet were illegible. Moreover, the contribution was the more perplexing at first as it opened with a succession of erased paragraphs. The writer appeared to have attempted the article once or twice in several journalistic styles. At the side of one experiment was written, 'Try American style,' and the fragment began—

'The King must go. We want gritty men. Flapdoodle is all very. . . . ;' and then broke off, followed by the note, 'Good sound journalism safer. Try it.'

The experiment in good sound journalism appeared to begin—

'The greatest of English poets has said that a rose by any. . . .'

This also stopped abruptly. The next annotation at the side was almost undecipherable, but seemed to be something like—

'How about old Steevens and the *mot juste*? E.g. . . .'

'Morning winked a little wearily at me over the curt edge of Campden Hill and its houses with their sharp shadows. Under the abrupt black cardboard of the outline, it took some little time to detect colours; but at length I saw a brownish yellow shifting in the obscurity, and I knew that it was the guard of Swindon's West Kensington army. They are being held as a reserve, and lining the whole ridge above the Bayswater Road. Their camp and their main force is under the great water works tower on Campden Hill. I forgot to say that the water works tower looked swart.

'As I passed them and came over the curve of Silver Street, I saw the blue cloudy masses of Barker's men blocking the entrance to the high road like a sapphire smoke (good). The disposition of the allied troops, under the general management of Mr. Wilson, appears to be as follows—The Yellow Army (if I may so describe the West Kensingtonians) lies, as I have said, in a strip along the ridge; its furthest point westward being the west side of Campden Hill Road, its furthest point eastward the beginning of Kensington Gardens. The Green Army of Wilson lines the Notting Hill High Road itself from Queen's Road to the corner of Pembridge Road, curving round the latter, and extending some three hundred yards up towards Westbourne Grove. Westbourne Grove itself is occupied by Barker of South Kensington. The fourth side of this rough square, the Queen's Road side, is held by some of Buck's Purple warriors.

'The whole resembles some ancient and dainty Dutch flower-bed. Along the crest of Campden Hill lie the golden crocuses of West Kensington. They are, as it were, the first fiery fringe of the whole. Northward lies our hyacinth Barker, with all his blue hyacinths. Round to the southwest run the green rushes of Wilson of Bayswater, and a line of violet irises (aptly symbolised by Mr. Buck) complete the whole. The argent exterior . . . (I am losing the

style. I should have said "Curving with a whisk" instead
of merely "Curving." Also I should have called the
hyacinths "sudden." I cannot keep this up. War is too
rapid for this style of writing. Please ask the office-boy to
insert *mots justes*.)

'The truth is that there is nothing to report. That
commonplace element which is always ready to devour all
beautiful things (as the Black Pig in the Irish Mythology
will finally devour the stars and gods); that commonplace
element, as I say, has in its Black Piggish way devoured
finally the chances of any romance in this affair; that which
once consisted of absurd but thrilling combats in the streets,
has degenerated into something which is the very prose of
warfare—it has degenerated into a siege. A siege may be
defined as a peace plus the inconvenience of war. Of course
Wayne cannot hold out. There is no more chance of help
from anywhere else than of ships from the moon. And if
old Wayne had stocked his street with tinned meats till all
his garrison had to sit on them, he couldn't hold out for
more than a month or two. As a matter of melancholy fact
he has done something rather like this. He has stocked his
street with food until there must be uncommonly little
room to turn round. But what is the good? To hold out
for all that time and then to give in of necessity, what does
it mean? It means waiting until your victories are forgotten
and then taking the trouble to be defeated. I cannot understand how Wayne can be so inartistic.

'And how odd it is that one views a thing quite differ-
ently when one knows it is defeated. I always thought
Wayne was rather fine. But now, when I know that he is
done for, there seems to be nothing else but Wayne. All
the streets seem to point at him, all the chimneys seem to

lean towards him. I suppose it is a morbid feeling; but Pump Street seems to be the only part of London that I feel physically. I suppose, I say, that it is morbid. I suppose it is exactly how a man feels about his heart when his heart is weak. "Pump Street"—the heart is a pump. And I am drivelling.

'Our finest leader at the front is beyond all question, General Wilson. He has adopted alone among the other Provosts the uniform of his own halberdiers, although that fine old sixteenth-century garb was not originally intended to go with red side-whiskers. It was he who, against a most admirable and desperate defence, broke last night into Pump Street and held it for at least half an hour. He was afterwards expelled from it by General Turnbull, of Notting Hill, but only after desperate fighting and the sudden descent of that terrible darkness which proved so much more fatal to the forces of General Buck and General Swindon.

'Provost Wayne himself, with whom I had, with great good fortune, a most interesting interview, bore the most eloquent testimony to the conduct of General Wilson and his men. His precise words are as follows: "I have bought sweets at his funny little shop when I was four years old, and ever since. I never noticed anything, I am ashamed to say, except that he talked through his nose, and didn't wash himself particularly. And he came over our barricade like a devil from hell." I repeated this speech to General Wilson himself, with some delicate improvements, and he seemed pleased with it. He does not, however, seem pleased with anything so much just now as he is with the wearing of a sword. I have it from the front on the best authority that General Wilson was not completely shaved yesterday. It is believed in military circles that he is growing a moustache. . . .

'As I have said, there is nothing to report. I walk wearily to the pillar-box at the corner of Pembridge Road to post my copy. Nothing whatever has happened, except the preparations for a particularly long and feeble siege, during which I trust I shall not be required to be at the Front. As I glance up Pembridge Road in the growing dusk, the aspect of that road reminds me that there is one note worth adding. General Buck has suggested, with characteristic acumen, to General Wilson, that in order to obviate the possibility of such a catastrophe as overwhelmed the allied forces in the last advance on Notting Hill (the catastrophe, I mean, of the extinguished lamps), that each soldier should have a lighted lantern round his neck. This is one of the things which I really admire about General Buck. He possesses what people used to mean by "the humility of the man of science," that is, he learns steadily from his mistakes. Wayne may score off him in some other way, but not in that way. The lanterns look like fairy lights as they curve round the end of Pembridge Road.

'*Later.*—I write with some difficulty, because the blood will run down my face and make patterns on the paper. Blood is a very beautiful thing; that is why it is concealed. If you ask me why blood runs down my face, I can only reply that I was kicked by a horse. If you ask me what horse, I can reply with some pride that it was a war-horse. If you ask me how a war-horse came on the scene in our simple pedestrian warfare, I am reduced to the necessity, so painful to a special correspondent, of recounting my experiences.

'I was, as I have said, in the very act of posting my copy at the pillar-box, and of glancing as I did so up the glittering curve of Pembridge Road, studded with the lights of Wilson's men. I don't know what made me pause to examine the matter, but I had a fancy that the line of lights, where it melted into the indistinct brown twilight, was more indistinct than usual. I was almost certain that in a certain stretch of the road where there had been five lights there were now only four. I strained my eyes; I counted them again, and there were only three. A moment after there were only two; an instant after only one; and an instant after that the lanterns near to me swung like jangled bells, as if struck suddenly. They flared and fell; and for the moment the fall of them was like the fall of the sun and stars out of heaven. It left everything in a primal blindness. As a matter of fact, the road was not yet legitimately dark. There were still red rays of a sunset in the sky, and the brown gloaming was still warmed, as it were, with a feeling as of firelight. But for three seconds after the lanterns swung and sank, I saw in front of me a blackness blocking the sky. And with the fourth second I knew that this blackness which blocked the sky was a man on a great horse; and I was trampled and tossed aside as a swirl of horsemen swept round the corner. As they turned I saw that they were not black but scarlet; they were a sortie of the besieged, Wayne riding ahead.

'I lifted myself from the gutter, blinded with blood from a very slight skin-wound, and, queerly enough, not caring either for the blindness or for the slightness of the wound. For one mortal minute after that amazing cavalcade had spun past, there was dead stillness on the empty road. And then came Barker and all his halberdiers running like devils in

the track of them. It had been their business to guard the
gate by which the sortie had broken out; but they had not
reckoned, and small blame to them, on cavalry. As it was,
Barker and his men made a perfectly splendid run after
them, almost catching Wayne's horses by the tails.

'Nobody can understand the sortie. It consists only of a
small number of Wayne's garrison. Turnbull himself,
with the vast mass of it, is undoubtedly still barricaded in
Pump Street. Sorties of this kind are natural enough in the
majority of historical sieges, such as the siege of Paris in
1870, because in such cases the besieged are certain of some
support outside. But what can be the object of it in this
case? Wayne knows (or if he is too mad to know anything, at least Turnbull knows) that there is not, and never
has been, the smallest chance of support for him outside;
that the mass of the sane modern inhabitants of London
regard his farcical patriotism with as much contempt as
they do the original idiotcy that gave it birth—the folly of
our miserable King. What Wayne and his horsemen are
doing nobody can even conjecture. The general theory
round here is that he is simply a traitor, and has abandoned
the besieged. But all such larger but yet more soluble
riddles are as nothing compared to the one small but un-
answerable riddle: Where did they get the horses?

'*Later.*—I have heard a most extraordinary account of
the origin of the appearance of the horses. It appears that
that amazing person, General Turnbull, who is now ruling
Pump Street in the absence of Wayne, sent out, on the
morning of the declaration of war, a vast number of little
boys (or cherubs of the gutter, as we pressmen say), with
half-crowns in their pockets, to take cabs all over London.

No less than a hundred and sixty cabs met at Pump Street; were commandeered by the garrison. The men were set free, the cabs used to make barricades, and the horses kept in Pump Street, where they were fed and exercised for several days, until they were sufficiently rapid and efficient to be used for this wild ride out of the town. If this is so, and I have it on the best possible authority, the method of the sortie is explained. But we have no explanation of its object. Just as Barker's Blues were swinging round the corner after them, they were stopped, but not by an enemy; only by the voice of one man, and he a friend. Red Wilson of Bayswater ran alone along the main road like a madman, waving them back with a halberd snatched from a sentinel. He was in supreme command, and Barker stopped at the corner, staring and bewildered. We could hear Wilson's voice loud and distinct out of the dusk, so that it seemed strange that the great voice should come out of the little body. "Halt, South Kensington! Guard this entry, and prevent them returning. I will pursue. Forward, the Green Guards!"

'A wall of dark blue uniforms and a wood of poleaxes was between me and Wilson, for Barker's men blocked the mouth of the road in two rigid lines. But through them and through the dusk I could hear the clear orders and the clank of arms, and see the green army of Wilson marching by towards the west. They were our great fighting men. Wilson had filled them with his own fire; in a few days they had become veterans. Each of them wore a silver medal of a pump, to boast that they alone of all the allied armies had stood victorious in Pump Street.

'I managed to slip past the detachment of Barker's Blues, who are guarding the end of Pembridge Road, and a sharp spell of running brought me to the tail of Wilson's green army as it swung down the road in pursuit of the flying Wayne. The dusk had deepened into almost total darkness; for some time I only heard the throb of the marching pace. Then suddenly there was a cry, and the tall fighting men were flung back on me, almost crushing me, and again the lanterns swung and jingled, and the cold nozzles of great horses pushed into the press of us. They had turned and charged us.

'"You fools!" came the voice of Wilson, cleaving our panic with a splendid cold anger. "Don't you see? the horses have no riders!"

'It was true. We were being plunged at by a stampede of horses with empty saddles. What could it mean? Had Wayne met some of our men and been defeated? Or had he flung these horses at us as some kind of ruse or mad new mode of warfare, such as he seemed bent on inventing? Or did he and his men want to get away in disguise? Or did they want to hide in houses somewhere?

'Never did I admire any man's intellect (even my own) so much as I did Wilson's at that moment. Without a word, he simply pointed the halberd (which he still grasped) to the southern side of the road. As you know, the streets running up to the ridge of Campden Hill from the main road are peculiarly steep, they are more like sudden flights of stairs. We were just opposite Aubrey Road, the steepest of all; up that it would have been far more difficult to urge half-trained horses than to run up on one's feet.

'"Left wheel!" hallooed Wilson. "They have gone up here," he added to me, who happened to be at his elbow.

'"Why?" I ventured to ask.

'"Can't say for certain," replied the Bayswater General. "They've gone up here in a great hurry anyhow. They've simply turned their horses loose, because they couldn't take them up. I fancy I know. I fancy they're trying to get over the ridge to Kensington or Hammersmith, or somewhere, and are striking up here because it's just beyond the end of our line. Damned fools, not to have gone further along the road, though. They've only just shaved our last outpost. Lambert is hardly four hundred yards from here. And I've sent him word."

'"Lambert!" I said. "Not young Wilfrid Lambert— my old friend."

'"Wilfrid Lambert's his name," said the General; "used to be a 'man about town;' silly fellow with a big nose. That kind of man always volunteers for some war or other. And what's funnier, he generally isn't half bad at it. Lambert is distinctly good. The yellow West Kensingtons I always reckoned the weakest part of the army; but he has pulled them together uncommonly well, though he's subordinate to Swindon, who's a donkey. In the attack from Pembridge Road the other night he showed great pluck."

'"He has shown greater pluck than that," I said. "He has criticised my sense of humour. That was his first engagement."

'This remark was, I am sorry to say, lost on the admirable commander of the allied forces. We were in the act of climbing the last half of Aubrey Road, which is so abrupt a slope that it looked like an old-fashioned map leaning up against the wall. There are lines of little trees, one above the other, as in the old-fashioned map.

'We reached the top of it, panting somewhat, and were

just about to turn the corner by a place called (in chivalrous anticipation of our wars of sword and axe) Tower Crecy, when we were suddenly knocked in the stomach (I can use no other term) by a horde of men hurled back upon us. They wore the red uniform of Wayne; their halberds were broken; their foreheads bleeding; but the mere impetus of their retreat staggered us as we stood at the last ridge of the slope.

'"Good old Lambert!" yelled out, suddenly, the stolid Mr. Wilson of Bayswater, in an uncontrollable excitement. "Damned jolly old Lambert! He's got there already! He's driving them back on us! Hurrah! hurrah! Forward the Green Guards!"

'We swung round the corner eastwards, Wilson running first, brandishing the halberd.

'Will you pardon a little egotism? Every one likes a little egotism, when it takes the form, as mine does in this case, of a disgraceful confession. The thing is really a little interesting, because it shows how the merely artistic habit has bitten into men like me. It was the most intensely exciting occurrence that had ever come to me in my life; and I was really intensely excited about it. And yet, as we turned that corner, the first impression I had was of something that had nothing to do with the fight at all. I was stricken from the sky as by a thunderbolt, by the height of the Waterworks Tower on Campden Hill. I don't know whether Londoners generally realise how high it looks when one comes out in this way, almost immediately under it. For the second it seemed to me that at the foot of it even human war was a triviality. For the second I felt as if I had been drunk with some trivial orgie, and that I had been sobered by the shock of that shadow. A moment afterwards, I realised that under it was going on something more enduring than stone, and something wilder than the dizziest height—the agony of man. And I knew that compared to that, this overwhelming tower was itself a triviality; it was a mere stalk of stone which humanity could snap like a stick.

'I don't know why I have talked so much about this silly old Waterworks Tower, which at the very best was only a tremendous background. It was that, certainly, a sombre and awful landscape, against which our figures were relieved. But I think the real reason was, that there was in my own mind so sharp a transition from the tower of stone to the man of flesh. For what I saw first when I had shaken off, as it were, the shadow of the tower, was a man, and a man I knew.

'Lambert stood at the further corner of the street that curved round the tower, his figure outlined in some degree by the beginning of moonrise. He looked magnificent, a hero; but he looked something much more interesting than that. He was, as it happened, in almost precisely the same swaggering attitude in which he had stood nearly fifteen years ago, when he swung his walking-stick and struck it into the ground, and told me that all my subtlety was drivel. And, upon my soul, I think he required more courage to say that than to fight as he does now. For then he was fighting against something that was in the ascendant, fashionable, and victorious. And now he is fighting (at the risk of his life, no doubt) merely against something which is already dead, which is impossible, futile; of which nothing has been more impossible and futile than this very sortie which has brought him into contact with it. People nowadays allow infinitely too little for the psychological sense

F

of victory as a factor in affairs. Then he was attacking the degraded but undoubtedly victorious Quin; now he is attacking the interesting but totally extinguished Wayne.

'His name recalls me to the details of the scene. The facts were these. A line of red halberdiers, headed by Wayne, were marching up the street, close under the northern wall, which is, in fact, the bottom of a sort of dyke, or fortification of the Waterworks. Lambert and his yellow West Kensingtons had that instant swept round the corner and had shaken the Waynites heavily, hurling back a few of the more timid, as I have just described, into our very arms. When our force struck the tail of Wayne's, every one knew that all was up with him. His favourite military barber was struck down. His grocer was stunned. He himself was hurt in the thigh, and reeled back against the wall. We had him in a trap with two jaws. "Is that you?" shouted Lambert, genially, to Wilson, across the hemmed-in host of Notting Hill. "That's about the ticket," replied General Wilson; "keep them under the wall."

'The men of Notting Hill were falling fast. Adam Wayne threw up his long arms to the wall above him, and with a spring stood upon it, a gigantic figure against the moon. He tore the banner out of the hands of the standard-bearer below him, and shook it out suddenly above our heads, so that it was like thunder in the heavens.

'"Round the Red Lion!" he cried. "Swords round the Red Lion! Halberds round the Red Lion! They are the thorns round the rose."

'His voice and the crack of the banner made a momentary rally, and Lambert, whose idiotic face was almost beautiful with battle, felt it as by an instinct, and cried—

'"Drop your public-house flag, you footler! Drop it!"

'"The banner of the Red Lion seldom stoops," said Wayne, proudly, letting it out luxuriantly on the night wind.

'The next moment I knew that poor Adam's sentimental theatricality had cost him much. Lambert was on the wall at a bound, his sword in his teeth, and had slashed at Wayne's head before he had time to draw his sword, his hands being busy with the enormous flag. He stepped back only just in time to avoid the first cut, and let the flag-staff fall, so that the spear-blade at the end of it pointed to Lambert.

'"The banner stoops," cried Wayne, in a voice that must have startled streets. "The banner of Notting Hill stoops to a hero." And with the words he drove the spear-point and half the flag-staff through Lambert's body and dropped him dead upon the road below, a stone upon the stones of the street.

'"Notting Hill! Notting Hill!" cried Wayne, in a sort of divine rage. "Her banner is all the holier for the blood of a brave enemy! Up on the wall, patriots! Up on the wall! Notting Hill!"

'With his long strong arm he actually dragged a man up on to the wall to be silhouetted against the moon, and more and more men climbed up there, pulled themselves and were pulled, till clusters and crowds of the half-massacred men of Pump Street massed up on the wall above us.

'"Notting Hill! Notting Hill!" cried Wayne, unceasingly.

'"Well, what about Bayswater?" said a worthy working-man in Wilson's army, irritably. "Bayswater for ever!"

'"We have won!" cried Wayne, striking his flag-staff

in the ground. "Bayswater for ever! We have taught our
enemies patriotism!"

'"Oh, cut these fellows up and have done with it!" cried
one of Lambert's lieutenants, who was reduced to something bordering on madness by the responsibility of suc-
ceeding to the command.

'"Let us by all means try," said Wilson, grimly; and the
two armies closed round the third.

.   .   .   .   .   .

'I simply cannot describe what followed. I am sorry,
but there is such a thing as physical fatigue, as physical
nausea, and, I may add, as physical terror. Suffice it to say
that the above paragraph was written about 11 p.m., and
that it is now about 2 a.m., and that the battle is not
finished, and is not likely to be. Suffice it further to say
that down the steep streets which lead from the Waterworks Tower to the Notting Hill High Road, blood
has been running, and is running, in great red serpents,
that curl out into the main thoroughfare and shine in the
moon.

'*Later.*—The final touch has been given to all this terrible
futility. Hours have passed; morning has broken; men are
still swaying and fighting at the foot of the tower and round
the corner of Aubrey Road; the fight has not finished. But
I know it is a farce.

'News has just come to show that Wayne's amazing
sortie, followed by the amazing resistance through a whole
night on the wall of the Waterworks, is as if it had not been.
What was the object of that strange exodus we shall
probably never know, for the simple reason that every one

who knew will probably be cut to pieces in the course of the next two or three hours.

'I have heard, about three minutes ago, that Buck and Buck's methods have won after all. He was perfectly right, of course, when one comes to think of it, in holding that it was physically impossible for a street to defeat a city. While we thought he was patrolling the eastern gates with his Purple army; while we were rushing about the streets and waving halberds and lanterns; while poor old Wilson was scheming like Moltke and fighting like Achilles to entrap the wild Provost of Notting Hill,—Mr. Buck, retired draper, has simply driven down in a hansom cab and done something about as plain as butter and about as useful and nasty. He has gone down to South Kensington, Brompton, and Fulham, and by spending about four thousand pounds of his private means, has raised an army of nearly as many men; that is to say, an army big enough to beat, not only Wayne, but Wayne and all his present enemies put together. The army, I understand, is encamped along High Street, Kensington, and fills it from the Church to Addison Road Bridge. It is to advance by ten different roads uphill to the north.

'I cannot endure to remain here. Everything makes it worse than it need be. The dawn, for instance, has broken round Campden Hill; splendid spaces of silver, edged with gold, are torn out of the sky. Worse still, Wayne and his men feel the dawn; their faces, though bloody and pale, are strangely hopeful . . . insupportably pathetic. Worst of all, for the moment they are winning. If it were not for Buck and the new army they might just, and only just, win.

'I repeat, I cannot stand it. It is like watching that won-

derful play of old Maeterlinck's (you know my partiality
for the healthy, jolly old authors of the nineteenth century),
in which one has to watch the quiet conduct of people
inside a parlour, while knowing that the very men are
outside the door whose word can blast it all with tragedy.
And this is worse, for the men are not talking, but writhing
and bleeding and dropping dead for a thing that is already
settled—and settled against them. The great grey masses of
men still toil and tug and sway hither and thither around
the great grey tower; and the tower is still motionless, as it
will always be motionless. These men will be crushed before the sun is set; and new men will arise and be crushed,
and new wrongs done, and tyranny will always rise again
like the sun, and injustice will always be as fresh as the
flowers of spring. And the stone tower will always look
down on it. Matter, in its brutal beauty, will always look
down on those who are mad enough to consent to die,
and yet more mad, since they consent to live.'

Thus ended abruptly the first and last contribution of the
Special Correspondent of the *Court Journal* to that valued
periodical.

The Correspondent himself, as has been said, was simply
sick and gloomy at the last news of the triumph of Buck.
He slouched sadly down the steep Aubrey Road, up which
he had the night before run in so unusual an excitement,
and strolled out into the empty dawn-lit main road, looking
vaguely for a cab. He saw nothing in the vacant space
except a blue-and-gold glittering thing, running very fast,
which looked at first like a very tall beetle, but turned out,
to his great astonishment, to be Barker.

'Have you heard the good news?' asked that gentleman.

'Yes,' said Quin, with a measured voice. 'I have heard the glad tidings of great joy. Shall we take a hansom down to Kensington? I see one over there.'

They took the cab, and were, in four minutes, fronting the ranks of the multitudinous and invincible army. Quin had not spoken a word all the way, and something about him had prevented the essentially impressionable Barker from speaking either.

The great army, as it moved up Kensington High Street, called many heads to the numberless windows, for it was long indeed—longer than the lives of most of the tolerably young—since such an army had been seen in London. Compared with the vast organisation which was now swallowing up the miles, with Buck at its head as leader, and the King hanging at its tail as journalist, the whole story of our problem was insignificant. In the presence of that army the red Notting Hills and the green Bayswaters were alike tiny and straggling groups. In its presence the whole struggle round Pump Street was like an ant-hill under the hoof of an ox. Every man who felt or looked at that infinity of men knew that it was the triumph of Buck's brutal arithmetic. Whether Wayne was right or wrong, wise or foolish, was quite a fair matter for discussion. But it was a matter of history. At the foot of Church Street, opposite Kensington Church, they paused in their glowing good humour.

'Let us send some kind of messenger or herald up to them,' said Buck, turning to Barker and the King. 'Let us send and ask them to cave in without more muddle.'

'What shall we say to them?' said Barker, doubtfully.

'The facts of the case are quite sufficient,' rejoined Buck. 'It is the facts of the case that make an army surrender. Let us simply say that our army that is fighting their army, and their army that is fighting our army, amount altogether to about a thousand men. Say that we have four thousand. It is very simple. Of the thousand fighting, they have at the very most, three hundred, so that, with those three hundred, they have now to fight four thousand seven hundred men. Let them do it if it amuses them.'

And the Provost of North Kensington laughed.

The herald who was despatched up Church Street in all the pomp of the South Kensington blue and gold, with the Three Birds on his tabard, was attended by two trumpeters.

'What will they do when they consent?' asked Barker, for the sake of saying something in the sudden stillness of that immense army.

'I know my Wayne very well,' said Buck laughing. 'When he submits he will send a red herald flaming with the Lion of Notting Hill. Even defeat will be delightful to him, since it is formal and romantic.'

The King, who had strolled up to the head of the line, broke silence for the first time.

'I shouldn't wonder,' he said, 'if he defied you, and didn't send the herald after all. I don't think you do know your Wayne quite so well as you think.'

'All right, your Majesty,' said Buck, easily; 'if it isn't disrespectful, I'll put my political calculations in a very simple form. I'll lay you ten pounds to a shilling the herald comes with the surrender.'

'All right,' said Auberon. 'I may be wrong, but it's my notion of Adam Wayne that he'll die in his city, and that, till he is dead, it will not be a safe property.'

'The bet's made, your Majesty,' said Buck.

Another long silence ensued, in the course of which Barker alone, amid the motionless army, strolled and stamped in his restless way.

Then Buck suddenly leant forward.

'It's taking your money, your Majesty,' he said. 'I knew it was. There comes the herald from Adam Wayne.'

'It's not,' cried the King, peering forward also. 'You brute, it's a red omnibus.'

'It's not,' said Buck, calmly; and the King did not answer, for down the centre of the spacious and silent Church Street was walking, beyond question, the herald of the Red Lion, with two trumpeters.

Buck had something in him which taught him how to be magnanimous. In his hour of success he felt magnanimous towards Wayne, whom he really admired; magnanimous towards the King, off whom he had scored so publicly; and, above all, magnanimous towards Barker, who was the titular leader of this vast South Kensington army, which his own talent had evoked.

'General Barker,' he said, bowing, 'do you propose now to receive the message from the besieged?'

Barker bowed also, and advanced towards the herald.

'Has your master, Mr. Adam Wayne, received our request for surrender?' he asked.

The herald conveyed a solemn and respectful affirmative.

Barker resumed, coughing slightly, but encouraged.

'What answer does your master send?'

The herald again inclined himself submissively, and answered in a kind of monotone.

'My message is this. Adam Wayne, Lord High Provost of Notting Hill, under the charter of King Auberon and the laws of God and all mankind, free and of a free city,

G

greets James Barker, Lord High Provost of South Kensington, by the same rights free and honourable, leader of the army of the South. With all friendly reverence, and with all constitutional consideration, he desires James Barker to lay down his arms, and the whole army under his command to lay down their arms also.'

Before the words were ended the King had run forward into the open space with shining eyes. The rest of the staff and the forefront of the army were literally struck breathless. When they recovered they began to laugh beyond restraint; the revulsion was too sudden.

'The Lord High Provost of Notting Hill,' continued the herald, 'does not propose, in the event of your surrender, to use his victory for any of those repressive purposes which others have entertained against him. He will leave you your free laws and your free cities, your flags and your governments. He will not destroy the religion of South Kensington, or crush the old customs of Bayswater.'

An irrepressible explosion of laughter went up from the forefront of the great army.

'The King must have had something to do with this humour,' said Buck, slapping his thigh. 'It's too deliciously insolent. Barker, have a glass of wine.'

And in his conviviality he actually sent a soldier across to the restaurant opposite the church and brought out two glasses for a toast.

When the laughter had died down, the herald continued quite monotonously—

'In the event of your surrendering your arms and dispersing under the superintendence of our forces, these local rights of yours shall be carefully observed. In the event of your not doing so, the Lord High Provost of Notting Hill

desires to announce that he has just captured the Waterworks Tower, just above you, on Campden Hill, and that
within ten minutes from now, that is, on the reception
through me of your refusal, he will open the great reservoir
and flood the whole valley where you stand in thirty feet
of water. God save King Auberon!'

Buck had dropped his glass and sent a great splash of
wine over the road.

'But—but——' he said; and then by a last and splendid
effort of his great sanity, looked the facts in the face.

'We must surrender,' he said. 'You could do nothing
against fifty thousand tons of water coming down a steep
hill, ten minutes hence. We must surrender. Our four
thousand men might as well be four. *Vicisti Gelilæe!* Per-
kins, you may as well get me another glass of wine.'

In this way the vast army of South Kensington surrendered and the Empire of Notting Hill began. One further
fact in this connection is perhaps worth mentioning—the
fact that, after his victory, Adam Wayne caused the great
tower on Campden Hill to be plated with gold and inscribed with a great epitaph, saying that it was the monument of Wilfrid Lambert, the heroic defender of the place,
and surmounted with a statue, in which his large nose was
done something less than justice to.

BOOK FIVE

CHAPTER I

The Empire of Notting Hill

ON the evening of the third of October, twenty years after the great victory of Notting Hill, which gave it the dominion of London, King Auberon came, as of old, out of Kensington Palace.

He had changed little, save for a streak or two of grey in his hair, for his face had always been old, and his step slow, and, as it were, decrepit.

If he looked old, it was not because of anything physical or mental. It was because he still wore, with a quaint conservatism, the frock-coat and high hat of the days before the great war. 'I have survived the Deluge,' he said. 'I am a pyramid, and must behave as such.'

As he passed up the street the Kensingtonians, in their picturesque blue smocks, saluted him as a King, and then looked after him as a curiosity. It seemed odd to them that men had once worn so elvish an attire.

The King, cultivating the walk attributed to the oldest inhabitant ('Gaffer Auberon' his friends were now confidentially desired to call him), went toddling northward. He paused, with reminiscence in his eye, at the Southern Gate of Notting Hill, one of those nine great gates of bronze and steel, wrought with reliefs of the old battles, by the hand of Chiffy himself.

'Ah!' he said, shaking his head and assuming an unnecessary air of age, and a provincialism of accent, 'Ah! I mind when there warn't none of this here.'

He passed through the Ossington Gate, surmounted by a great lion, wrought in red copper on yellow brass, with the motto, 'Nothing Ill.' The guard in red and gold saluted him with his halberd.

It was about sunset, and the lamps were being lit. Auberon paused to look at them, for they were Chiffy's finest work, and his artistic eye never failed to feast on them. In memory of the Great Battle of the Lamps, each great iron lamp was surmounted by a veiled figure, sword in hand, holding over the flame an iron hood or extinguisher, as if ready to let it fall if the armies of the South and West should again show their flags in the city. Thus no child in Notting Hill could play about the streets without the very lamp-posts reminding him of the salvation of his country in the dreadful year.

'Old Wayne was right in a way,' commented the King. 'The sword does make things beautiful. It has made the whole world romantic by now. And to think people once thought me a buffoon for suggesting a romantic Notting Hill. Deary me, deary me (I think that is the expression). It seems like a previous existence.'

Turning a corner he found himself in Pump Street, opposite the four shops which Adam Wayne had studied twenty years before. He entered idly the shop of Mr. Mead, the grocer. Mr. Mead was somewhat older, like the rest of the world, and his red beard, which he now wore with a moustache, and long and full, was partly blanched and discoloured. He was dressed in a long and richly embroidered robe of blue, brown, and crimson, interwoven with an Eastern complexity of pattern, and

covered with obscure symbols and pictures, representing
his wares passing from hand to hand and from nation to
nation. Round his neck was the chain with the Blue
Argosy cut in turquoise, which he wore as Grand Master
of the Grocers. The whole shop had the sombre and sump-
tuous look of its owner. The wares were displayed as
prominently as in the old days, but they were now blended
and arranged with a sense of tint and grouping, too often
neglected by the dim grocers of those forgotten days. The
wares were shown plainly, but shown not so much as an
old grocer would have shown his stock, but rather as an
educated virtuoso would have shown his treasures. The
tea was stored in great blue and green vases, inscribed with
the nine indispensable sayings of the wise men of China.
Other vases of a confused orange and purple, less rigid and
dominant, more humble and dreamy, stored symbolically
the tea of India. A row of caskets of a simple silvery metal
contained tinned meats. Each was wrought with some
rude but rhythmic form, as a shell, a horn, a fish, or an
apple, to indicate what material had been canned in it.

'Your Majesty,' said Mr. Mead, sweeping an Oriental
reverence. 'This is an honour to me, but yet more an
honour to the city.'

Auberon took off his hat.

'Mr. Mead,' he said, 'Notting Hill, whether in giving or
taking, can deal in nothing but honour. Do you happen to
sell liquorice?'

'Liquorice, sire,' said Mr. Mead, 'is not the least important of our benefits out of the dark heart of Arabia.'

And going reverently towards a green and silver canister,
made in the form of an Arabian mosque, he proceeded to
serve his customer.

'I was just thinking, Mr. Mead,' said the King reflectively, 'I don't know why I should think about it just now, but I was just thinking of twenty years ago. Do you remember the times before the war?'

The grocer, having wrapped up the liquorice sticks in a piece of paper (inscribed with some appropriate sentiment), lifted his large grey eyes dreamily, and looked at the darkening sky outside.

'Oh yes, your Majesty,' he said. 'I remember these streets before the Lord Provost began to rule us. I can't remember how we felt very well. All the great songs and the fighting change one so; and I don't think we can really estimate all we owe to the Provost; but I can remember his coming into this very shop twenty-two years ago, and I remember the things he said. The singular thing is that as far as I remember I thought the things he said odd at that time. Now it's the things that I said, as far as I can recall them, that seem to me odd—as odd as a madman's antics.'

'Ah!' said the King; and looked at him with an unfathomable quietness.

'I thought nothing of being a grocer then,' he said. 'Isn't that odd enough for anybody? I thought nothing of all the wonderful places that my goods come from, and wonderful ways that they are made. I did not know that I was for all practical purposes a king with slaves spearing fishes near the secret-pool, and gathering fruits in the islands under the world. My mind was a blank on the thing. I was as mad as a hatter.'

The King turned also, and stared out into the dark, where the great lamps that commemorated the battle were already flaming.

'And is this the end of poor old Wayne?' he said, half to

himself. 'To inflame every one so much that he is lost himself in the blaze. Is this his victory, that he, my incomparable Wayne, is now only one in a world of Waynes? Has he conquered and become by conquest commonplace? Must Mr. Mead, the grocer, talk as high as he? Lord! what a strange world in which a man cannot remain unique even by taking the trouble to go mad.'

And he went dreamily out of the shop.

He paused outside the next one almost precisely as the Provost had done two decades before.

'How uncommonly creepy this shop looks,' he said. 'But yet somehow encouragingly creepy, invitingly creepy. It looks like something in a jolly old nursery story in which you are frightened out of your skin, and yet know that things always end well. The way those low sharp gables are carved like great black bat's wings folded down, and the way those queer-coloured bowls underneath are made to shine like giant's eye-balls. It looks like a benevolent warlock's hut. It is apparently a chemist's.'

Almost as he spoke, Mr. Bowles, the chemist, came to his shop door in a long black velvet gown and hood, monastic as it were, but yet with a touch of the diabolic. His hair was still quite black, and his face even paler than of old. The only spot of colour he carried was a red star cut in some precious stone of strong tint, hung on his breast. He belonged to the Society of the Red Star of Charity, founded on the lamps displayed by doctors and chemists.

'A fine evening, sir,' said the chemist. 'Why, I can scarcely be mistaken in supposing it to be your Majesty. Pray step inside and share a bottle of sal-volatile, or anything that may take your fancy. As it happens there is an old acquaintance of your Majesty's in my shop carousing (if I may be permitted the term) upon that beverage at this moment.'

The King entered the shop, which was an Aladdin's garden of shades and hues, for as the chemist's scheme of colour was more brilliant than the grocer's scheme, so it was arranged with even more delicacy and fancy. Never, if the phrase may be employed, had such a nosegay of medicines been presented to the artistic eye.

But even the solemn rainbow of that evening interior was rivalled or even eclipsed by the figure standing in the centre of the shop. His form, which was a large and stately one, was clad in a brilliant blue velvet, cut in the richest Renaissance fashion, and slashed so as to show gleams and gaps of a wonderful lemon or pale yellow. He had several chains round his neck and his plumes, which were of several tints of bronze and gold, hung down to the great gold hilt of his long sword. He was drinking a dose of sal-volatile, and admiring its opal tint. The King advanced with a slight mystification towards the tall figure, whose face was in shadow, then he said—

'By the Great Lord of Luck, Barker!'

The figure removed his plumed cap, showing the same dark head and long, almost equine, face which the King had so often seen rising out of the high collar of Bond Street. Except for a grey patch on each temple, it was totally unchanged.

'Your Majesty,' said Barker, 'this is a meeting nobly retrospective, a meeting that has about it a certain October gold. I drink to old days;' and he finished his sal-volatile with simple feeling.

'I am delighted to see you again, Barker,' said the King.

G*

'It is, indeed, long since we met. What with my travels in Asia Minor, and my book having to be written (you have read my "Life of Prince Albert for Children," of course), we have scarcely met twice since the Great War. That is twenty years ago.'

'I wonder,' said Barker, thoughtfully, 'if I might speak freely to your Majesty.'

'Well,' said Auberon, 'it's rather late in the day to start speaking respectfully. Flap away, my bird of freedom.'

'Well, your Majesty,' replied Barker, lowering his voice, 'I don't think it will be so long to the next war.'

'What do you mean?' asked Auberon.

'We will stand this insolence no longer,' burst out Barker, fiercely. 'We are not slaves because Adam Wayne twenty years ago cheated us with a water-pipe. Notting Hill is Notting Hill; it is not the world. We in South Kensington, we also have memories—aye, and hopes. If they fought for these trumpery shops and a few lamp-posts, shall we not fight for the great High Street and the sacred Natural History Museum?'

'Great Heavens!' said the astounded Auberon. 'Will wonders never cease? Have the two greatest marvels been achieved? Have you turned altruistic, and has Wayne turned selfish? Are you the patriot, and he the tyrant?'

'It is not from Wayne himself altogether that the evil comes,' answered Barker. 'He, indeed, is now mostly wrapped in dreams, and sits with his old sword beside the fire. But Notting Hill is the tyrant, your Majesty. Its Council and its crowds have been so intoxicated by the spreading over the whole city of Wayne's old ways and visions, that they try to meddle with every one, and rule every one, and civilise every one, and tell every one what is good for him. I do not deny the great impulse which his old war, wild as it seemed, gave to the civic life of our time. It came when I was still a young man, and I admit it enlarged my career. But we are not going to see our own cities flouted and thwarted from day to day because of something Wayne did for us all nearly a quarter of a century ago. I am just waiting here for news upon this very matter. It is rumoured that Notting Hill has vetoed the statue of General Wilson they are putting up opposite Chepstow Place. If that is so, it is a black and white shameless breach of the terms on which we surrendered to Turnbull after the battle of the Tower. We were to keep our own customs and self-government. If that is so——'

'It is so,' said a deep voice; and both men turned round.

A burly figure in purple robes, with a silver eagle hung round his neck and moustaches almost as florid as his plumes, stood in the doorway.

'Yes,' he said, acknowledging the King's start, 'I am Provost Buck, and the news is true. These men of the Hill have forgotten that we fought round the Tower as well as they did, and that it is sometimes foolish, as well as base, to despise the conquered.'

'Let us step outside,' said Barker, with a grim composure.

Buck did so, and stood rolling his eyes up and down the lamp-lit street.

'I would like to have a go at smashing all this,' he muttered, 'though I am over sixty. I would like——'

His voice ended in a cry, and he reeled back a step, with his hands to his eyes, as he had done in those streets twenty years before.

'Darkness!' he cried—'darkness again! What does it mean?'

For in truth every lamp in the street had gone out, so that they could not see even each other's outline, except faintly. The voice of the chemist came with startling cheerfulness out of the density.

'Oh, don't you know?' he said. 'Did they never tell you this is the Feast of the Lamps, the anniversary of the great battle that almost lost and just saved Notting Hill? Don't you know, your Majesty, that on this night twenty-one years ago we saw Wilson's green uniforms charging down this street, and driving Wayne and Turnbull back upon the gas-works, fighting with their handful of men like fiends from hell? And that then, in that great hour, Wayne sprang through a window of the gas-works, with one blow of his hand brought darkness on the whole city, and then with a cry like a lion's, that was heard through four streets, flew at Wilson's men, sword in hand, and swept them, bewildered as they were, and ignorant of the map, clear out of the sacred street again? And don't you know that upon that night every year all lights are turned out for half an hour while we sing the Notting Hill anthem in the darkness? Hark! there it begins.'

Through the night came a crash of drums, and then a strong swell of human voices—

'When the world was in the balance, there was night on Notting Hill,
(There was night on Notting Hill): it was nobler than the day;
On the cities where the lights are and the firesides glow,
From the seas and from the deserts came the thing we did not know,
Came the darkness, came the darkness, came the darkness on the foe,
    And the old guard of God turned to bay.
For the old guard of God turns to bay, turns to bay,

And the stars fall down before it ere its banners fall to-day.
For when armies were around us as a howling and a horde,
When falling was the citadel and broken was the sword,
The darkness came upon them like the Dragon of the Lord,
When the old guard of God turned to bay.'

The voices were just uplifting themselves in a second
verse, when they were stopped by a scurry and a yell.
Barker bounded into the street with a cry of 'South
Kensington!' and a drawn dagger. In less time than man
could blink, the whole packed street was full of curses and
struggling. Barker was flung back against the shop-front,
but used the second only to draw his sword as well as his
dagger, and calling out, 'This is not the first time I've come
through the thick of you,' flung himself again into the
press. It was evident that he had drawn blood at last, for
a more violent outcry arose, and many other knives and
swords were discernible in the faint light. Barker, after
having wounded more than one man, seemed on the point
of being flung back again, when Buck suddenly stepped out
into the street. He had no weapon, for he affected rather
the peaceful magnificence of the great burgher, than the
pugnacious dandyism which had replaced the old sombre
dandyism in Barker. But with a blow of his clenched fist
he broke the pane of the next shop, which was the old
curiosity shop, and, plunging in his hand, snatched a kind
of Japanese scimitar, and calling out, 'Kensington! Kensington!' rushed to Barker's assistance.

Barker's sword was broken, but he was laying about him
with his dagger. Just as Buck ran up, a man of Notting
Hill struck Barker down, but Buck struck the man down
on top of him, and Barker sprang up again, the blood
running down his face.

Suddenly all these cries were cloven by a great voice, that seemed to fall out of heaven. It was terrible to Buck and Barker and the King from its seeming to come out of the empty skies; but it was more terrible because it was a familiar voice, and one which at the same time they had not heard for so long.

'Turn up the lights,' said the voice from above them, and for a moment there was no reply, but only a tumult.

'In the name of Notting Hill, and of the great Council of the City, turn up the lights.'

There was again a tumult and a vagueness for a moment, then the whole street and every object in it sprang suddenly out of the darkness, as every lamp sprang into life. And looking up they saw, standing upon a balcony near the roof of one of the highest houses, the figure and the face of Adam Wayne, his red hair blowing behind him, a little streaked with grey.

'What is this, my people?' he said. 'Is it altogether impossible to make a thing good without it immediately insisting on being wicked? The glory of Notting Hill in having achieved its independence, has been enough for me to dream of for many years, as I sat beside the fire. Is it really not enough for you, who have had so many other affairs to excite and distract you? Notting Hill is a nation. Why should it condescend to be a mere Empire? You wish to pull down the statue of General Wilson, which the men of Bayswater have so rightly erected in Westbourne Grove. Fools! Who erected that statue? Did Bayswater erect it? No. Notting Hill erected it. Do you not see that it is the glory of our achievement that we have infected the other cities with the idealism of Notting Hill? It is we who have created not only our own side, but both sides of this controversy. O too humble fools—why should you wish to destroy your enemies? You have done something more to them. You have created your enemies. You wish to pull down that gigantic silver hammer, which stands, like an obelisk, in the centre of the Broadway of Hammersmith. Fools! Before Notting Hill arise, did any person passing through Hammersmith Broadway expect to see there a gigantic silver hammer? You wish to abolish the great bronze figure of a knight standing upon the artificial bridge at Knightsbridge. Fools! Who would have thought of it before Notting Hill arose? I have even heard, and with deep pain I have heard it, that the evil eye of our imperial envy has been cast towards the remote horizon of the west, and that we have objected to the great black monument of a crowned raven, which commemorates the skirmish of Ravenscourt Park. Who created all these things? Were they there before we came? Cannot you be content with that destiny which was enough for Athens, which was enough for Nazareth? the destiny, the humble purpose of creating a new world. Is Athens angry because Romans and Florentines have adopted her phraseology for expressing their own patriotism? Is Nazareth angry because as a little village it has become the type of all little villages out of which, as the Snobs say, no good can come? Has Athens asked every one to wear the chlamys? Are all the followers of the Nazarene compelled to wear turbans? No! but the soul of Athens went forth and made men drink hemlock, and the soul of Nazareth went forth and made men consent to be crucified. So has the soul of Notting Hill gone forth and made men realise what it is to live in a city. Just as we inaugurated our symbols and ceremonies, so they have inaugurated theirs; and are you

so mad as to contend against them? Notting Hill is right;
it has always been right. It has moulded itself on its own
necessities, its own *sine quâ non,* it has accepted its own
ultimatum. Because it is a nation it has created itself. And
because it is a nation it can destroy itself. Notting Hill
shall always be the judge. If it is your will because of this
matter of General Wilson's statue to make war upon
Bayswater——'

A roar of cheers broke in upon his words, and further
speech was impossible. Pale to the lips, the great patriot
tried again and again to speak; but even his authority could
not keep down the dark and roaring masses in the street
below him. He said something further, but it was not
audible. He descended at last sadly from the garret in
which he lived, and mingled with the crowd at the foot of
the houses. Finding General Turnbull, he put his hand on
his shoulder with a queer affection and gravity, and said—

'To-morrow, old man, we shall have a new experience,
as fresh as the flowers of spring. We shall be defeated. You
and I have been through three battles together, and have
somehow or other missed this peculiar delight. It is un-
fortunate that we shall not probably be able to exchange
our experiences, because, as it most annoyingly happens,
we shall probably both be dead.'

Turnbull looked dimly surprised.

'I don't mind so much about being dead,' he said, 'but
why should you say that we shall be defeated?'

'The answer is very simple,' replied Wayne, calmly. 'It
is because we ought to be defeated. We have been in the
most horrible holes before now; but in all those I was perfectly certain that the stars were on our side, and that we
ought to get out. Now, I know that we ought not to get

out; and that takes away from me everything with which I won.'

As Wayne spoke he started a little, for both men became aware that a third figure was listening to them—a small figure with wondering eyes.

'Is it really true, my dear Wayne,' said the King, interrupting, 'that you think you will be beaten to-morrow?'

'There can be no doubt about it whatever,' replied Adam Wayne; 'the real reason is the one of which I have just spoken. But as a concession to your materialism, I will add that they have an organised army of a hundred allied cities against our one. That in itself, however, would be unimportant.'

Quin, with his round eyes, seemed strangely insistent.

'You are quite sure,' he said, 'that you must be beaten?'

'I am afraid,' said Turnbull, gloomily, 'that there can be no doubt about it.'

'Then,' cried the King, flinging out his arms, 'give me a halberd! Give me a halberd, somebody! I desire all men to witness that I, Auberon, King of England, do here and now abdicate and implore the Provost of Notting Hill to permit me to enlist in his army. Give me a halberd!'

He seized one from some passing guard, and, shouldering it, stamped solemnly after the shouting columns of halberdiers which were, by this time, parading the streets. He had, however, nothing to do with the wrecking of the statue of General Wilson, which took place before morning.

CHAPTER II

The Last Battle

THE day was cloudy when Wayne went down to die with all his army in Kensington Gardens; it was cloudy again when that army had been swallowed up by the vast armies of a new world. There had been an almost uncanny interval of sunshine, in which the Provost of Notting Hill, with all the placidity of an onlooker, had gazed across to the hostile armies on the great spaces of verdure opposite; the long strips of green and blue and gold lay across the park in squares and oblongs like a proposition in Euclid wrought in a rich embroidery. But the sunlight was a weak and, as it were, a wet sunlight, and was soon swallowed up. Wayne spoke to the King, with a queer sort of coldness and languor, as to the military operations. It was as he had said the night before, that being deprived of his sense of an impracticable rectitude he was, in effect, being deprived of everything. He was out of date, and at sea in a mere world of compromise and competition, of Empire against Empire, of the tolerably right and the tolerably wrong. When his eye fell on the King, however, who was marching very gravely with a top hat and a halberd, it brightened slightly.

'Well, your Majesty,' he said, 'you at least ought to be proud to-day. If your children are fighting each other, at least those who win are your children. Other kings have distributed justice, you have distributed life. Other kings have ruled a nation, you have created nations. Others have made kingdoms, you have begotten them. Look at your children, father.' And he stretched his hand out towards the enemy.

Auberon did not raise his eyes.

'See how splendidly,' cried Wayne, 'the new cities come on—the new cities from across the river. See where Battersea advances over there—under the flag of the Lost Dog; and Putney—don't you see the Man on the White Boar shining on their standard as the sun catches it? It is the coming of a new age, your Majesty. Notting Hill is not a common empire; it is a thing like Athens, the mother of a mode of life, of a manner of living, which shall renew the youth of the world—a thing like Nazareth. When I was young I remember, in the old dreary days, wiseacres used to write books about how trains would get faster, and all the world would be one empire, and tram-cars go to the moon. And even as a child I used to say to myself, "Far more likely that we shall go on the crusades again, or worship the gods of the city." And so it has been. And I am glad, though this is my last battle.'

Even as he spoke there came a crash of steel from the left, and he turned his head.

'Wilson!' he cried, with a kind of joy. 'Red Wilson has charged our left. No one can hold him in; he eats swords. He is as keen a soldier as Turnbull, but less patient—less really great. Ha! and Barker is moving. How Barker has improved; how handsome he looks. It is not all having plumes; it is also having a soul in one's daily life. Ha!'

And another crash of steel on the right showed that Barker had closed with Notting Hill on the other side.

'Turnbull is there!' cried Wayne. 'See him hurl them

back! Barker is checked! Turnbull charges—wins! But our left is broken. Wilson has smashed Bowles and Mead, and may turn our flank. Forward, the Provost's Guard!'

And the whole centre moved forward, Wayne's face and hair and sword flaming in the van.

The King ran suddenly forward.

The next instant a great jar that went through it told that it had met the enemy. And right over against them through the wood of their own weapons Auberon saw the Purple Eagle of Buck of North Kensington.

On the left Red Wilson was storming the broken ranks, his little green figure conspicuous even in the tangle of men and weapons, with the flaming red moustaches and the crown of laurel. Bowles slashed at his head and tore away some of the wreath, leaving the rest bloody, and, with a roar like a bull's, Wilson sprang at him, and, after a rattle of fencing, plunged his point into the chemist, who fell, crying 'Notting Hill!' Then the Notting Hillers wavered, and Bayswater swept them back in confusion. Wilson had carried everything before him.

On the right, however, Turnbull had carried the Red Lion banner with a rush against Barker's men, and the banner of the Golden Birds bore up with difficulty against it. Barker's men fell fast. In the centre Wayne and Buck were engaged, stubborn and confused. So far as the fighting went, it was precisely equal. But the fighting was a farce. For behind the three small armies with which Wayne's small army was engaged lay the great sea of the allied armies, which looked on as yet as scornful spectators, but could have broken all four armies by moving a finger.

Suddenly they did move. Some of the front contingents, the pastoral chiefs from Shepherd's Bush, with their spears and fleeces, were seen advancing, and the rude clans from Paddington Green. They were advancing for a very good reason. Buck, of North Kensington, was signalling wildly; he was surrounded, and totally cut off. His regiments were a struggling mass of people, islanded in a red sea of Notting Hill.

The allies had been too careless and confident. They had allowed Barker's force to be broken to pieces by Turnbull, and the moment that was done, the astute old leader of Notting Hill swung his men round and attacked Buck behind and on both sides. At the same moment Wayne cried 'Charge!' and struck him in front like a thunderbolt.

Two-thirds of Buck's men were cut to pieces before their allies could reach them. Then the sea of cities came on with their banners like breakers, and swallowed Notting Hill for ever. The battle was not over, for not one of Wayne's men would surrender, and it lasted till sundown, and long after. But it was decided; the story of Notting Hill was ended.

When Turnbull saw it, he ceased a moment from fighting, and looked round him. The evening sunlight struck his face; it looked like a child's.

'I have had my youth,' he said. Then snatching an axe from a man, he dashed into the thick of the spears of Shepherd's Bush, and died somewhere far in the depths of their reeling ranks. Then the battle roared on; every man of Notting Hill was slain before night.

Wayne was standing by a tree alone after the battle. Several men approached him with axes. One struck at him. His foot seemed partly to slip; but he flung his hand out, and steadied himself against the tree.

Barker sprang after him, sword in hand, and shaking with excitement.

'How large now, my lord,' he cried, 'is the Empire of Notting Hill?'

Wayne smiled in the gathering dark.

'Always as large as this,' he said, and swept his sword round in a semi-circle of silver.

Barker dropped, wounded in the neck; and Wilson sprang over his body like a tiger-cat, rushing at Wayne. At the same moment there came behind the Lord of the Red Lion a cry and a flare of yellow, and a mass of the West Kensington halberdiers ploughed up the slope, knee-deep in grass, bearing the yellow banner of the city before them, and shouting aloud.

At the same second Wilson went down under Wayne's sword, seemingly smashed like a fly. The great sword rose again like a bird, but Wilson seemed to rise with it, and, his sword being broken, sprang at Wayne's throat like a dog. The foremost of the yellow halberdiers had reached the tree and swung his axe above the struggling Wayne. With a curse the King whirled up his own halberd and dashed the blade in the man's face. He reeled, and rolled down the slope, just as the furious Wilson was flung on his back again. And again he was on his feet, and again at Wayne's throat. Then he was flung again, but this time laughing triumphantly. Grasped in his hand was the red and yellow favour that Wayne wore as Provost of Notting Hill. He had torn it from the place where it had been carried for twenty-five years.

With a shout the West Kensington men closed round Wayne, the great yellow banner flapping over his head.

'Where is your favour now, Provost?' cried the West Kensington leader.

And a laugh went up.

Adam struck at the standard-bearer and brought him reeling forward. As the banner stopped, he grasped the yellow folds and tore off a shred. A halberdier struck him on the shoulder, wounding bloodily.

'Here is one colour!' he cried, pushing the yellow into his belt; 'and here!' he cried, pointing to his own blood, 'Here is the other.'

At the same instant the shock of a sudden and heavy halberd laid the King stunned or dead. In the wild visions of vanishing consciousness, he saw again something that belonged to an utterly forgotten time, something that he had seen somewhere long ago in a restaurant. He saw, with his swimming eyes, red and yellow, the colours of Nicaragua.

Quin did not see the end. Wilson, wild with joy, sprang again at Adam Wayne, and the great sword of Notting Hill was whirled above once more. Then men ducked instinctively at the rushing noise of the sword coming down out of the sky, and Wilson of Bayswater was smashed and wiped down upon the floor like a fly. Nothing was left of him but a wreck; but the blade that had broken him was broken. In dying he had snapped the great sword and the spell of it; the sword of Wayne was broken at the hilt. One rush of the enemy carried Wayne by force against the tree. They were too close to use halberd or even sword; they were breast to breast, even nostrils to nostrils. But Buck got his dagger free.

'Kill him!' he cried, in a strange stifled voice. 'Kill him! Good or bad, he is none of us! Do not be blinded by the

face. . . ! God! have we not been blinded all along!' and
he drew his arm back for a stab and seemed to close his
eyes.

Wayne did not drop the hand that hung on to the tree-
branch. But a mighty heave went over his breast and his
whole huge figure, like an earthquake over great hills. And
with that convulsion of effort he rent the branch out of the
tree, with tongues of torn wood. And swaying it once
only, he let the splintered club fall on Buck, breaking his
neck. The planner of the Great Road fell face foremost
dead, with his dagger in a grip of steel.

'For you and me, and for all brave men, my brother,'
said Wayne, in his strange chant, 'there is good wine
poured in the inn at the end of the world.'

The packed men made another lurch or heave towards
him; it was almost too dark to fight clearly. He caught
hold of the oak again, this time getting his hand into a wide
crevice and grasping, as it were, the bowels of the tree.
The whole crowd, numbering some thirty men, made a
rush to tear him away from it; they hung on with all their
weight and numbers, and nothing stirred. A solitude could
not have been stiller than that group of straining men.
Then there was a faint sound.

'His hand is slipping,' cried two men in exultation.

'You don't know much of him,' said another, grimly
(a man of the old war). 'More likely his bone cracks.'

'It is neither—by God, it is neither!' said one of the first
two.

'What is it, then?' asked the second.

'The tree is falling,' he replied.

'As the tree falleth, so shall it lie,' said Wayne's voice out
of the darkness, and it had the same sweet and yet horrible

air that it had had throughout, of coming from a great
distance, from before or after the event. Even when he was
struggling like an eel or battering like a madman, he spoke
like a spectator. 'As the tree falleth, so shall it lie,' he said.
'Men have called that a gloomy text. It is the essence of all
exultation. I am doing now what I have done all my life,
what is the only happiness, what is the only universality.
I am clinging to something. Let it fall, and there let it lie.
Fools, you go about and see the kingdoms of the earth, and
are liberal, and wise, and cosmopolitan, which is all that
the devil can give you—all that he could offer to Christ only
to be spurned away. I am doing what the truly wise do.
When a child goes out into the garden and takes hold of a
tree, saying, "Let this tree be all I have," that moment its
roots take hold on hell and its branches on the stars. The
joy I have is what the lover knows when a woman is
everything. It is what a savage knows when his idol is
everything. It is what I know when Notting Hill is everything. I have a city. Let it stand or fall.'

As he spoke, the turf lifted itself like a living thing, and
out of it rose slowly, like crested serpents, the roots of the
oak. Then the great head of the tree, that seemed a green
cloud among grey ones, swept the sky suddenly like a
broom, and the whole tree heeled over like a ship, smashing
every one in its fall.

CHAPTER III

Two Voices

IN a place in which there was total darkness for hours, there was also for hours total silence. Then a voice spoke out of the darkness, no one could have told from where, and said aloud—

'So ends the Empire of Notting Hill. As it began in blood, so it ended in blood, and all things are always the same.'

And there was silence again, and then again there was a voice, but it had not the same tone; it seemed that it was not the same voice.

'If all things are always the same, it is because they are always heroic. If all things are always the same, it is because they are always new. To each man one soul only is given; to each soul only is given a little power—the power at some moments to outgrow and swallow up the stars. If age after age that power comes upon men, whatever gives it to them is great. Whatever makes men feel old is mean—an empire or a skin-flint shop. Whatever makes men feel young is great—a great war or love story. And in the darkest of the books of God there is written a truth that is also a riddle. It is of the new things that men tire—of fashions and proposals and improvements and change. It is the old things that startle and intoxicate. It is the old things that are young. There is no sceptic who does not feel that many have doubted before. There is no rich and fickle man who does not feel that all his novelties are ancient. There is no worshipper of change who does not feel upon his neck the vast weight of the weariness of the universe. But we who do the old things are fed by nature with a perpetual infancy. No man who is in love

thinks that any one has been in love before. No woman
who has a child thinks that there have been such things as
children. No people that fight for their own city are
haunted with the burden of the broken empires. Yes, oh
dark voice, the world is always the same, for it is always
unexpected.'

A little gust of wind blew through the night, and then
the first voice answered—

'But in this world there are some, be they wise or
foolish, whom nothing intoxicates. There are some who
see all your disturbances like a cloud of flies. They know
that while men will laugh at your Notting Hill, and will
study and rehearse and sing of Athens and Jerusalem,
Athens and Jerusalem were silly suburbs like your Notting
Hill. They know that the earth itself is a suburb, and can
feel only drearily and respectably amused as they move
upon it.'

'They are philosophers or they are fools,' said the other
voice. 'They are not men. Men live, as I say, rejoicing
from age to age in something fresher than progress—in the
fact that with every baby a new sun and a new moon
are made. If our ancient humanity were a single man, it
might perhaps be that he would break down under the
memory of so many loyalties, under the burden of so
many diverse heroisms, under the load and terror of all the
goodness of men. But it has pleased God so to isolate the
individual soul that it can only learn of all other souls by
hearsay, and to each one goodness and happiness come with
the youth and violence of lightning, as momentary and as
pure. And the doom of failure that lies on all human
systems does not in real fact affect them any more than the
worms of the inevitable grave affect a children's game in a
meadow. Notting Hill has fallen; Notting Hill has died.

But that is not the tremendous issue. Notting Hill has lived.'

'But if,' answered the other voice, 'if what is achieved by all these efforts be only the common contentment of humanity, why do men so extravagantly toil and die in them? Has nothing been done by Notting Hill that any chance clump of farmers or clan of savages would not have done without it? What might have been done to Notting Hill if the world had been different may be a deep question; but there is a deeper. What could have happened to the world if Notting Hill had never been?'

The other voice replied—

'The same that would have happened to the world and all the starry systems if an apple-tree grew six apples instead of seven; something would have been eternally lost. There has never been anything in the world absolutely like Notting Hill. There will never be anything quite like it to the crack of doom. I cannot believe anything but that God loved it as He must surely love anything that is itself and unreplaceable. But even for that I do not care. If God, with all His thunders, hated it, I loved it.'

And with the voice a tall, strange figure lifted itself out of the *débris* in the half-darkness.

The other voice came after a long pause, and as it were hoarsely.

'But suppose the whole matter were really a hocus-pocus. Suppose that whatever meaning you may choose in your fancy to give to it, the real meaning of the whole was mockery. Suppose it was all folly. Suppose——'

'I have been in it,' answered the voice from the tall and strange figure, 'and I know it was not.'

A smaller figure seemed half to rise in the dark.

'Suppose I am God,' said the voice, 'and suppose I made

the world in idleness. Suppose the stars, that you think eternal, are only the idiot fireworks of an everlasting schoolboy. Suppose the sun and the moon, to which you sing alternately, are only the two eyes of one vast and sneering giant, opened alternately in a never-ending wink. Suppose the trees, in my eyes, are as foolish as enormous toad-stools. Suppose Socrates and Charlemagne are to me only beasts, made funnier by walking on their hind legs. Suppose I am God, and having made things, laugh at them.'

'And suppose I am man,' answered the other. 'And suppose that I give the answer that shatters even a laugh. Suppose I do not laugh back at you, do not blaspheme you, do not curse you. But suppose, standing up straight under the sky, with every power of my being, I thank you for the fools' paradise you have made. Suppose I praise you, with a literal pain of ecstasy, for the jest that has brought me so terrible a joy. If we have taken the child's games, and given them the seriousness of a Crusade, if we have drenched your grotesque Dutch garden with the blood of martyrs, we have turned a nursery into a temple. I ask you, in the name of Heaven, who wins?'

The sky close about the crest of the hills and trees was beginning to turn from black to grey, with a random suggestion of the morning. The slight figure seemed to crawl towards the larger one, and the voice was more human.

'But suppose, friend,' it said, 'suppose that, in a bitterer and more real sense, it was all a mockery. Suppose that there had been, from the beginning of these great wars, one who watched them with a sense that is beyond expression, a sense of detachment, of responsibility, of irony, of agony. Suppose that there were one who knew it was all a joke.'

The tall figure answered—

'He could not know it. For it was not all a joke.'

And a gust of wind blew away some clouds that sealed the sky-line, and showed a strip of silver behind his great dark legs. Then the other voice came, having crept nearer still.

'Adam Wayne,' it said, 'there are men who confess only *in articulo mortis*; there are people who blame themselves only when they can no longer help others. I am one of them. Here, upon the field of the bloody end of it all, I come to tell you plainly what you would never understand before. Do you know who I am?'

'I know you, Auberon Quin,' answered the tall figure, 'and I shall be glad to unburden your spirit of anything that lies upon it.'

'Adam Wayne,' said the other voice, 'of what I have to say you cannot in common reason be glad to unburden me. Wayne, it was all a joke. When I made these cities, I cared no more for them than I care for a centaur, or a merman, or a fish with legs, or a pig with feathers, or any other absurdity. When I spoke to you solemnly and encouragingly about the flag of your freedom and the peace of your city, I was playing a vulgar practical joke on an honest gentleman, a vulgar practical joke that has lasted for twenty years. Though no one could believe it of me perhaps, it is the truth that I am a man both timid and tenderhearted. I never dared in the early days of your hope, or the central days of your supremacy, to tell you this; I never dared to break the colossal calm of your face. God knows why I should do it now, when my farce has ended in tragedy and the ruin of all your people! But I say it now. Wayne, it was done as a joke.'

There was silence, and the freshening breeze blew the sky

clearer and clearer, leaving great spaces of the white dawn.

At last Wayne said, very slowly—

'You did it all only as a joke?'

'Yes,' said Quin.

'When you conceived the idea,' went on Wayne, dreamily, 'of an army for Bayswater and a flag for Notting Hill, there was no gleam, no suggestion in your mind that such things might be real and passionate?'

'No,' answered Auberon, turning his round, white face to the morning with a dull and splendid sincerity; 'I had none at all.'

Wayne sprang down from the height above him and held out his hand.

'I will not stop to thank you,' he said, with a curious joy in his voice, 'for the great good for the world you have actually wrought. All that I think of that I have said to you a moment ago, even when I thought that your voice was the voice of a derisive omnipotence, its laughter older than the winds of heaven. But let me say what is immediate and true. You and I, Auberon Quin, have both of us throughout our lives been again and again called mad. And we are mad. We are mad, because we are not two men but one man. We are mad, because we are two lobes of the same brain, and that brain has been cloven in two. And if you ask for the proof of it, it is not hard to find. It is not merely that you, the humourist, have been in these dark days stripped of the joy of gravity. It is not merely that I, the fanatic, have had to grope without humour. It is that though we seem to be opposite in everything, we have been opposite like man and woman, aiming at the same moment at the same practical thing. We are the father and the mother of the Charter of the Cities.'

Quin looked down at the *débris* of leaves and timber, the

relics of the battle and stampede, now glistening in the glowing daylight, and finally said—

'Yet nothing can alter the antagonism—the fact that I laughed at these things and you adored them.'

Wayne's wild face flamed with something god-like, as he turned it to be struck by the sunrise.

'I know of something that will alter that antagonism, something that is outside us, something that you and I have all our lives perhaps taken too little account of. The equal and eternal human being will alter that antagonism, for the human being sees no real antagonism between laughter and respect, the human being, the common man, whom mere geniuses like you and me can only worship like a god. When dark and dreary days come, you and I are necessary, the pure fanatic, the pure satirist. We have between us remedied a great wrong. We have lifted the modern cities into that poetry which every one who knows mankind knows to be immeasurably more common than the commonplace. But in healthy people there is no war between us. We are but the two lobes of the brain of a ploughman. Laughter and love are everywhere. The cathedrals, built in the ages that loved God, are full of blasphemous grotesques. The mother laughs continually at the child, the lover laughs continually at the lover, the wife at the husband, the friend at the friend. Auberon Quin, we have been too long separated; let us go out together. You have a halberd and I a sword, let us start our wanderings over the world. For we are its two essentials. Come, it is already day.'

In the blank white light Auberon hesitated a moment. Then he made the formal salute with his halberd, and they went away together into the unknown world.